THE BARK COVERED HOUSE

PREFATORY NOTE.

I little thought when I left my farm yards, horses and cattle in the care of other men, and began to write, that I should spend nearly all the winter of 1875 in writing; much less, that I should offer the product of such labor to the public, in the Centennial Year. But I have been urged to do so by many friends, both learned and unlearned, who have read the manuscript, or listened to parts of it. They think the work, although written by a farmer, should see the light and live for the information of others. One of these is Levi Bishop, of Detroit, who was long a personal friend of my father and his family, and has recently read the manuscript. He is now President of the "Wayne County Pioneer Society," and is widely known as a literary man, poet and author.

W.N.

KEY.

Sketch of the lives of John and Melinda Nowlin; of their journeying and settlement in Michigan.

Thrilling scenes and incidents of pioneer life, of hopes and fears, of ups and downs, of a life in the woods; continuing until the gloom and darkness of the forest were chased away, by the light of civilization, and the long battle for a home had been fought by the pioneer soldiers and they had gained a signal victory over nature herself.

Hope never forsook them in the darkest hours, but beckoned and cheered them on to the conquest of the wilderness. When that was consummated hope hovered and sat upon her pedestal of realization. For better days had come for the pioneers in the country they had found. Then was heard the joyful, enchanting "Harvest Home;" songs of "Peace and Plenty."

Crowned with honor, prosperity and happiness—for a time.

PREFACE.

I have delineated the scenes of this narrative, from time to time, as they took place. I thought at the time when they occurred that some of them were against me.

I do not place this volume before its readers that I may gain any applause: I have sought to say no more of myself than was necessary.

This is a labor of love, written to perpetuate the memory of some most noble lives, among whom were my father and mother who sought a home in the forests of Michigan at an early day. Being then quite young, I kept no record of dates or occurrences, and this book is mostly sketched from memory.

It is a history of my parents' struggles and triumphs in the wilderness. It ought to encourage all who read it, since not many begin life in a new country with fewer advantages than they.

It is said that "Truth is stranger than fiction." In this I have detailed the walks of ordinary life in the woods. In these pictures there is truth. All and more than I have said have been realized. My observations have been drawn from my own knowledge, in the main, but I am indebted to my sisters for some incidents related. Together, with our brother, we often sat around the clay hearth and listened to father's stories, words of encouragement and counsel. Together we shared and endured the fears, trials and hardships of a pioneer life.

This work cannot fail to be of deep interest to all persons of similar experience; and to their descendants for ages to come who can never too fully appreciate the blessings earned for them by their parents and others amid hardships, privations and sufferings (in a new country) the half of which can never be told.

CONTENTS

I.	TALKING OF MICHIGAN.	15
II.	DISAGREEABLE MUSIC.	25
III.	HOW WE GOT OUR SWEET, AND THE HISTORY OF MY FIRST PIG.	32
IV.	OUR SECOND HOUSE AND FIRST APPLE TREES.	39
V.	THE JUG OF WHISKY AND TEMPERANCE MEETING.	43
VI.	HOW WE FOUND OUR CATTLE.	47
VII.	TROUBLE CAME ON THE WING.	51
VIII.	HARD TIMES FOR US IN MICHIGAN, 1836-7.	53
IX.	A SUMMER HUNT.	56
X.	HOW WE GOT INTO TROUBLE ONE NIGHT, AND I SCARED.	61
XI.	THE INDIANS VISIT US—THEIR STRANGE AND PECULIAR WAYS.	65
XII.	THE INSIDE OF OUR HOUSE—A PICTURE FROM MEMORY.	73
XIII.	METHEGLIN OR THE DETECTED DRINK.	80
XIV.	OUR ROAD AND HOW I WAS WOUNDED.	86
XV.	PROSPECT OF WAR—A.D. 1835.	91
XVI.	FISHING AND BOATING.	98
XVII.	HOW I GOT IN TROUBLE RIDING IN A CANOE.	102
XVIII.	OUR CLEARING AND THE FIRST RAILROAD CARS IN 1838.	105
XIX.	TREES.	111

XX.	DRAWING CORD-WOOD—HOW THE RAILROAD WAS BUILT—THE STEAM WHISTLE.	117
XXI.	HOW I HUNTED AND WE PAID THE MORTGAGE.	123
XXII.	BEAR HUNT OF 1842.	132
XXIII.	GRANDFATHER'S POWDER-HORN—WAR WITH PIRATES.	140
XXIV.	LIGHT BEGINS TO DAWN.	148
XXV.	MAKING A BARGAIN.	153
XXVI.	HOW I COMMENCED FOR MYSELF—FATHER'S OLD FARM IN 1843.	157
XXVII.	THOUGHTS IN CONNECTION WITH FATHER AND EARLY PIONEER LIFE.	161
XXVIII.	FATHER'S NEW HOUSE AND ITS SITUATION—HIS CHILDREN VISIT HIM.	168
XXIX.	MY WATCH LOST AND VISIT TO CANADA.	175
XXX.	MOTHER'S VISIT TO THE EAST—1861.	184
XXXI.	LEAVING NEW YORK CITY FOR HOME.	194

CHAPTER I.

TALKING OF MICHIGAN.

My father was born in 1793, and my mother in 1802, in Putnam County, State of New York. Their names were John and Melinda Nowlin. Mother's maiden name was Light.

My father owned a small farm of twenty-five acres, in the town of Kent, Putnam County, New York, about sixty miles from New York City. We had plenty of fruit, apples, pears, quinces and so forth, also a never failing spring. He bought another place about half a mile from that. It was very stony, and father worked very hard. I remember well his building stone wall.

But hard work would not do it. He could not pay for the second place. It involved him so that we were in danger of losing the place where we lived.

He said, it was impossible for a poor man to get along and support his family; that he never could get any land for his children there, and he would sell what he had and go to a better country, where land was cheap and where he could get land for them.

He talked much of the territory of Michigan. He went to one of the neighbors and borrowed a geography. I recollect very well some things that it stated. It was Morse's geography, and it said that the territory of Michigan was a very fertile country, that it was nearly surrounded by great lakes, and that wild grapes and other wild fruit grew in abundance.

Father then talked continually of Michigan. Mother was very much opposed to leaving her home. I was the eldest of five children, about ten or eleven years of age, when the word Michigan grated upon my ear. I am not able to give dates in full, but all of the incidents I relate are facts. Some of them occurred over forty years ago, and are given mostly from memory, without the aid of a diary. Nevertheless, most of them are now more vivid and plain to my mind than some things which transpired within the past year. I was very much opposed to going to Michigan, and did all that a boy of my age could do to prevent it. The thought of Indians, bears and wolves terrified me, and the thought of leaving my schoolmates and native place was terrible. My parents sent me to school when in New York, but I have not been to school a day since. My mother's health was very poor. Her physician feared that consumption of the lungs was already seated. Many of her friends said she would not live to get to Michigan if she started. She thought she could not, and said, that if she did, herself and family would be killed by the Indians, perish in the wilderness, or starve to death. The thought too, of leaving her friends and the members of the church, to which she was very much attached, was terribly afflicting. She made one request of father, which was that when she died he would take her back to New York, and lay her in the grave yard by her ancestors.

Father had made up his mind to go to Michigan, and nothing could change him. He sold his place in 1832, hired a house for the summer, then went down to York, as we called it, to get his outfit. Among his purchases were a rifle for himself and a shot gun for me. He said when we went to Michigan it should be mine. I admired his rifle very much. It was the first one I had ever seen. After trying his rifle a few days, shooting at a mark, he bade us good-by, and started "to view" in Michigan.

I think he was gone six or eight weeks, when he returned and told us of his adventures and the country. He said he had a very hard time going up Lake Erie. A terrible storm caused the old boat, "Shelvin Thompson" to heave, and its timber to creak in almost every joint. He thought it must go down. He went to his friend, Mr. George Purdy, (who is now an old resident of the town of Dearborn) said to him: "You had better get up; we are going down! The Captain says 'every man on deck and look out for himself.'" Mr. Purdy was too sick to get up. The good old steamer weathered the storm and landed safely at Detroit.

Father said that Michigan was a beautiful country, that the soil was as rich as a barn-yard, as level as a house floor, and no stones in the way. (I here state, that he did not go any farther west than where he bought his land.) He also said he had bought eighty acres of land, in the town of Dearborn, two and a half miles from a little village, and twelve miles from the city of Detroit. Said he would buy eighty acres more, east of it, after he moved in the spring, which would make it square, a quarter section. He said it was as near Detroit as he could get government land, and he thought Detroit would always be the best market in the country.

Father had a mother, three sisters, one brother and an uncle living in Unadilla Country N.Y. He wished very much to see them, and, as they were about one hundred and fifty miles on his way to Michigan, he concluded to spend the winter with them. Before he was ready to start he wrote to his uncle, Griffin Smith, to meet him, on a certain day, at Catskill, on the Hudson river. I cannot give the exact date, but remember that it was in the fall of 1833.

The neighbor, of whom we borrowed the old geography, wished very much to go West with us, but could not raise the means. When we started we passed by his place; he was lying dead in his house. Thus were our hearts, already sad, made sadder.

We traveled twenty-five miles in a wagon, which brought us to Poughkeepsie, on the Hudson river, then took a night boat for Catskill where uncle was to meet us the next morning. Before we reached Catskill, the captain said that he would not stop there. Father said he must. The captain said he would not stop for a hundred dollars as his boat was behind time. But he and father had a little private conversation, and the result was he did stop. The captain told his men to be careful of the things, and we were helped off in the best style possible. I do not know what changed the captain's mind, perhaps he was a Mason. Uncle met us, and our things were soon on his wagon. Now, our journey lay over a rough, hilly country, and I remember it was very cold. I think we passed over some of the smaller Catskill Mountains. My delicate mother, wrapt as best she could be, with my little sister (not then a year old) in her arms, also the other children, rode. Father and I walked some of the way, as the snow was quite deep on the mountains. He carried his rifle, and I my shot-gun on our shoulders. Our journey was a tedious one, for we got along very slowly; but we finally arrived at Unadilla. There we had many friends and passed a pleasant winter. I liked the country better than the one we left, and we all tried to get father to buy there, and give up the idea of going to Michigan. But a few years satisfied us that he knew the best.

Early in the spring of 1834 we left our friends weeping, for, as they expressed it, they thought we were going "out of the world." Here I will give some lines composed and presented to father and mother by father's sister, N. Covey, which will give her idea of our undertaking better than any words I can frame:

"Dear Brother and Sister, we must bid you adieu,
We hope that the Lord will deal kindly with you,
Protect and defend you, wherever you go,
If Christ is your friend, sure you need fear no foe.

"The distance doth seem great, to which you are bound,
But soon we must travel on far distant ground,
And if we prove faithful to God's grace and love,
If we ne'er meet before, we shall all meet above."

About twenty years later this aunt, her husband and nine children (they left one son) sons-in-law, daughters-in-law and grand-children visited us. Uncle had sold his nice farm in Unadilla and come to settle his very intelligent family in Michigan. He settled as near us as he could get government land sufficient for so large a family. With most of this numerous family near him, he is at this day a sprightly old man, respected (so far as I know) by all who know him, from Unionville to Bay City.

Now as I have digressed, I must go back and continue the story of our journey from Unadilla to Michigan. As soon as navigation opened, in the spring, we started again with uncle's team and wagon. In this manner we traveled about fifty miles which brought us to Utica. There we embarked on a canal boat and moved slowly night and day, to invade the forests of Michigan. Sometimes when we came to a lock father got off and walked a mile or two. On one of these occasions I accompanied him, and when we came to a favorable place, father signaled to the steersman, and he turned the boat up. Father jumped on to the side of the boat. I attempted to follow him, did not jump far enough, missed my hold and went down, by the side of the boat, into the water. However, father caught my hand and lifted me out. They said that if he had not caught me, I must have been crushed to death, as the boat struck the side the same minute. That, certainly, would have been the end of my journey to Michigan. When it was pleasant we spent part of the time on deck. One day mother left my little brother, then four years old, in care of my oldest sister, Rachel. He concluded to have a rock in an easy chair, rocked over and took a cold bath in the canal. Mother and I were in the cabin. When we heard the cry "Overboard!" we rushed on deck, and the first thing we saw was a man swimming with something ahead of him. It proved to be my brother, held by one strong arm of an English gentleman. He did not strangle much; some said the Englishman might have waded out, in that case he would not have strangled any, as he had on a full-cloth overcoat, which held him up until the Englishman got to him. Be that as it may, the Englishman was our ideal hero for many years, for by his bravery and skill, unparalleled by anything we had seen, he had saved our brother from a watery grave.

That brother is now the John Smith Nowlin, of Dearborn.

Nothing more of importance occurred while we were on the canal. When we arrived at Buffalo the steamer, "Michigan," then new, just ready for her second trip, lay at her wharf ready to start the next morning. Thinking we would get a better night's rest, at a public house, than on the steamer father sought one, but made a poor choice.

Father had four or five hundred dollars, which were mostly silver, he thought this would be more secure and unsuspected in mother's willow basket, which would be thought to contain only wearing apparel for the child. We had just got nicely installed and father gone to make preparations for our embarkation on the "Michigan," when the lady of the house came by mother and, as if to move it a little, lifted her basket. Then she said, "You must have plenty of money, your basket is very heavy."

When father came, and mother told him the liberty the lady had taken, he did not like it much, and I am sure I felt anything but easy.

But father called for a sleeping room with three beds, and we were shown up three flights of stairs, into a dark, dismal room, with no window, and but one door. Mother saw us children in bed, put the basket of silver between my little brother and me, and then went down. The time seemed long, but finally father and mother came up. I felt much safer then. Late in the evening a man, with a candle in one hand, came into the room, looked at each bed sufficiently to see who was in it. When he came to father's bed, which proved to be the last, as he went round, father asked him what he wanted there. He said he was looking for an umbrella. Father said he would give him umbrella, caught him by the sleeve of his coat; but he proved to be stronger than his coat for he fled leaving one sleeve of a nice broadcloth coat in father's hand. Father then put his knife over the door-latch. I began to breathe more freely, but there was no sleep for father or mother, and but little for me, that night.

Everything had been quiet about two hours when we heard steps, as of two or three, coming very quietly, in their stocking feet. Father rose, armed himself with a heavy chair and waited to receive them.

Mother heard the door-latch, and fearing that father would kill, or be killed, spoke, as if not wishing them to hear, and said: "John have the pistols ready," (it will be remembered that we had pistols in place of revolvers in those days) "and the moment they open the door shoot them." This stratagem worked; they retired as still as possible.

In about two or three hours more, they came again, and although father told mother to keep still, she said again: "Be ready now and blow them down the moment they burst open the door."

Away they went again, but came once more just before daylight, stiller if possible than ever; father was at his station, chair in hand, but mother was determined all should live, if possible, so she said "They are coming again, shoot the first one that enters!" &c., &c.

They found that we were awake and, do doubt, thought that they would meet with a little warmer reception than they wished. Father really had no weapons with him except the chair and knife. I said, the room had no window, consequently, it was as dark at daylight as at midnight. The only way we could tell when it was daylight was by the noise on the street.

When father went down, in the morning, he inquired for the landlord and the man that came into his room; but the landlord and the man with one sleeve were not to be found. Father complained to the landlady, of being disturbed, and showed her the coatsleeve. She said it must have been an old man, who usually slept in that room, looking for a bed.

We went immediately to our boat. As father was poor and wished to economize, he took steerage passage, as we had warm clothes and plenty of bedding, he thought this the best that he could afford. Our headquarters were on the lower deck. In a short time steam was up, and we bade farewell to Buffalo, where we had spent a sleepless night, and with about six-hundred passengers started on our course.

The elements seemed to be against us. A fearful storm arose; the captain thought it would be dangerous to proceed, and so put in below a little island opposite Cleveland, and tied up to a pier which ran out from the island. Here we lay for three weary days and nights, the storm continually raging.

Finally, the captain thought he must start out. He kept the boat as near the shore as he could with safety, and we moved slowly until we were near the head of the lake. Then the storm raged and the wind blew with increased fury. It seemed as if the "Prince of the power of the air" had let loose the wind upon us. The very air seemed freighted with woe. The sky above and the waters below were greatly agitated. It was a dark afternoon, the clouds looked black and angry and flew across the horizon apparently in a strife to get away from the dreadful calamity that seemed to be coming upon Lake Erie.

We were violently tempest-tossed. Many of the passengers despaired of getting through. Their lamentations were piteous and all had gloomy forebodings of impending ruin. The dark, blue, cold waves, pressed hard by the wind, rolled and tumbled our vessel frightfully, seeming to make our fears their sport. What a dismal, heart-rending scene! After all our efforts in trying to reach Michigan, now I expected we must be lost. Oh how vain the expectation of reaching our new place, in the woods! I thought we should never see it. It looked to me as though Lake Erie would terminate our journey.

It seemed as if we were being weighed in a great balance and that wavering and swaying up and down; balanced about equally between hope and fear, life and death.

No one could tell which way it would turn with us. I made up my mind, and promised if ever I reached terra-firma never to set foot on that lake again; and I have kept my word inviolate. I was miserably sick, as were nearly all the passengers. I tried to keep on my feet, as much as I could; sometimes I would take hold of the railing and gaze upon the wild terrific scene, or lean against whatever I could find, that was stationary, near mother and the rest of the family. Mother was calm, but I knew she had little hope that we would ever reach land. She said, her children were all with her and we should not be parted in death; that we should go together, and escape the dangers and tribulations of the wilderness.

I watched the movements of the boat as much as I could. It seemed as if the steamer could not withstand the furious powers that were upon her. The front part of the boat would seem to settle down—down—lower and lower if possible than it had been before. It looked to me, often, as though we were going to plunge headforemost—alive, boat and all into the deep. After a while the boat would straighten herself again and hope revive for a moment; then I thought that our staunch boat was nobly contending with the adverse winds and waves, for the lives of her numerous passengers. The hope of her being able to outride the storm was all the hope I had of ever reaching shore.

I saw the Captain on deck looking wishfully toward the land, while the white-caps broke fearfully on our deck. The passengers were in a terrible state of consternation. Some said we gained a little headway; others said we did not. The most awful terror marked nearly every face. Some wept, some prayed, some swore and a few looked calm and resigned. I was trying to read my fate in other faces when an English lady, who came on the canal boat with us, and who had remained in the cabin up to this, time, rushed on deck, wringing her hands and crying at the top of her voice, "We shall be lost! we shall be lost! oh! oh! oh! I have crossed the Atlantic Ocean three times, and it never commenced with this! We shall be lost! oh! oh! oh!"

One horse that stood on the bow of the boat died from the effects of the storm. Our clothes and bedding were all drenched, and to make our condition still more perilous, the boat was discovered to be on fire. This was kept as quiet as possible. I did not know that it was burning, until after it was extinguished; but I saw father, with others, carrying buckets of water. He said the boat had been on fire and they had put it out. The staunch boat resisted the elements; ploughed her way through and landed us safely at Detroit.

Some years after our landing at Detroit, I saw the steamboat "Michigan" and thought of the perilous time we had on her coming up Lake Erie. She was then an old boat, and was laid up. I thought of the many thousand hardy pioneers she had brought across the turbulent lake and landed safely on the shore of the territory whose name she bore.

But where, oh where "are the six hundred!" that came on her with us? Most of them have bid adieu to earth, and all its storms. The rest of them are now old and no doubt scattered throughout the United States. But time or distance cannot erase from their memory or mine the storm we shared together on Lake Erie.

CHAPTER II.

DISAGREEABLE MUSIC.

It was night, in the Spring of 1834, when we arrived at Detroit, and we made our way to the "United States Hotel" which stood near where the old post office was and where the "Mariner's Church" now stands, on Woodbridge street.

The next morning I was up early and went to view the city. I wished to know if it was really a city. If it looked like Utica or Buffalo.

I went up Jefferson Avenue; found some brick buildings, barber poles, wooden clocks, or large watches, big hats and boots, a brass ball, &c., &c.

I returned to the Hotel, satisfied that Detroit was actually a city, for the things I had seen were, in my mind, sufficient to make it one. After I assured myself that there was a city, so far from New York, I was quite contented and took my breakfast. Then, with our guns on our shoulders, father and I started to see our brand-new farm at Dearborn. First we went up Woodward Avenue to where the new City Hall now stands, it was then only a common, dotted by small wooden buildings.

Thence we took the Chicago road which brought us to Dearbornville. From there the timber had been cut for a road one mile south. On this road father did his first road work in Michigan and here afterwards I helped to move the logs out. The road-master, Mr. Smith, was not willing to allow full time, for my work; however I put in part time. Little did I think that here, one mile from Dearbornville, father would, afterwards, buy a farm, build a large brick house, and end his days, in peace and plenty.

From this point, one mile south of the little village, we were one mile from father's chosen eighty, but had to follow an Indian trail two miles, which led us to Mr. J. Pardee's. His place joined father's on the west. We crossed Pardee's place, eighty rods, which brought us to ours. I dug up some of the earth, found it black and rich, and sure enough no stones in the way. Late in the afternoon I started back to mother, to tell her that father had engaged a Mr. Thompson (who kept tavern in a log house, half a mile east of Dearbornville) and team, and would come after her in the morning. When I reached the Chicago road again, it seemed anything but inviting. I could just see a streak ahead four or five miles, with the trees standing thick and dark either side.

If ever a boy put in good time I did then. However, it was evening when I reached Detroit, and I had traveled more than twenty-six miles. Mother was very glad to see me, and listened with interest, to her boy's first story of Michigan. I told her that father was coming in the morning, as he had said; that Mr. Joseph Pardee said, we could stay with him while we were building. I told her I was glad we came, how nice the land was, what a fine country it would be in a few years, and, with other comforting words, said, if we lived, I would take her back in a few years, to visit her old home.

The next morning father and Mr. Thompson came, and we were soon all aboard the wagon. When we reached Mr. Pardee's his family seemed very much pleased to see us. He said: "Now we have 'Old Put' here, we'll have company."

Putnam county joined the county he came from, and he called father "Old Put" because he came from Putnam county.

Father immediately commenced cutting logs for a house. In one week he had them ready, and men came from Dearbornville to help him raise them. He then cut black ash trees, peeled off the bark to roof his house, and after having passed two weeks under Mr. Pardee's hospitable roof, we moved into a house of our own, had a farm of our own and owed no one.

Father brought his axe from York State; it weighed seven pounds; he gave me a smaller one. He laid the trees right and left until we could see the sun from ten o'clock in the morning till between one and two in the afternoon, when it mostly disappeared back of Mr. Pardee's woods.

Father found it was necessary for him to have a team, so he went to Detroit and bought a yoke of oxen; also, at the same time, a cow. He paid eighty dollars for the oxen and twenty-five for the cow. These cattle were driven in from Ohio. The cow proved to be a great help toward the support of the family for a number of years. The oxen were the first owned in the south part of the town of Dearborn. They helped to clear the logs from the piece father had cut over, and we planted late corn, potatoes and garden stuff. The corn grew very high but didn't ear well. The land was indeed very rich, but shaded too much.

The next thing, after planting some seeds, was clearing a road through a black ash swale and flat lands on our west section line, running north one mile, which let us out to the point mentioned, one mile south of Dearbornville. We blazed the section line trees over, cleared out the old logs and brush, then felled trees lengthwise towards each other, sometimes two together, to walk on over the water; we called it our log-way. We found the country was so very wet, at times, that it was impossible to go with oxen and sled, which were our only means of conveyance, summer or winter. When we could not go in this style we were obliged to carry all that it was necessary to have taken, on our shoulders, from Dearbornville.

We had many annoyances, and mosquitoes were not the least, but they did us some good. We had no fences to keep our cattle, and the mosquitoes drove the oxen and cow up to the smoke which we kept near the house in order to keep those little pests away. The cattle soon learned, as well as we, that smoke was a very powerful repellant of those little warriors. Many times, in walking those logs and going through the woods there would be a perfect cloud of mosquitoes around me. Sometimes I would run to get away from them, then stop and look behind me and there would be a great flock for two rods back (beside those that were around me) all coming toward me as fast as their wings could bring them, and seeming only satisfied when they got to me. But they were cannibals and wanted to eat me. All sang the same song in the same old tune. I was always glad when I got out of their company into our own little clearing.

But Mr. Pardee was a little more brave; he said it was foolish to notice such small things as mosquitoes. I have seen them light on his face and run in their bills, probe in until they reached the fountain of life, suck and gormandize until they got a full supply, then leisurely fly away with their veins and bodies full of the best and most benevolent blood, to live awhile, and die from the effects of indulging too freely and taking too much of the life of another. Thus at different times I saw him let them fill themselves and go away without his seeming to notice them; whether he always treated them thus well or not, I cannot say, but I do know they were the worst of pests. Myriads of them could be found any where in the woods, that would eagerly light on man or beast and fill themselves till four times their common size, if they could get a chance. The woods were literally alive with them. No one can tell the wearisome sleepless hours they caused us at night. I have lain listening and waiting for them to light on my face or hands, and then trying to slap them by guess in the dark, sometimes killing them, and sometimes they would fly away, to come again in a few minutes. I could hear them as they came singing back. Frequently when I awoke I found them as wakeful as ever; they had been feasting while I slept. I would find bunches and blotches on me, wherever they had had a chance to light, which caused a disagreeable, burning and smarting sensation.

Frequently some one of us would get up and make a smudge in the room to quiet them; we did it by making a little fire of small chips and dirt, or by burning some sugar on coals, but this would only keep them still for a short time. These vexatious, gory-minded, musical-winged, bold denizens of the shady forest, were more eager to hold their carniverous feasts at twilight or in the night than any other time. In cloudy weather they were very troublesome as all the first settlers know. We had them many years, until the country was cleared and the land ditched; then, with the forest, they nearly disappeared.

As I have said our oxen were the first in our part of the town. Mr. Pardee had no team. Father sold him half of our oxen. They used them alternately, each one two weeks, during the summer. For some reason, Mr. Pardee failed to pay the forty dollars and when winter came father had to take the oxen back and winter them. The winter was very open, and much pleasanter than any we had ever seen. The cattle lived on what we called "French-bogs" which grew all through the woods on the low land and were green all winter.

We found wild animals and game very numerous. Sometimes the deer came where father had cut down trees, and browsed the tops. Occasionally, in the morning, after a little snow, their tracks would be as thick as sheep-tracks in a yard, almost up to the house. The wolves also, were very common; we could often hear them at night, first at one point, then answers from another and another direction, until the woods rang with their unearthly yells.

One morning I saw a place by a log where a deer had lain, and noticed a large quantity of hair all around on the snow; then I found tracks where two wolves came from the west, jumped over the log, and caught the deer in his bed. He got away, but he must have had bare spots on his back.

One evening a Mr. Bruin called at our house and stood erect at our north window. The children thought him one of us, as father, mother and I were away, and they ran out to meet us, but discovered instead a large black bear. When they ran out, Mr. Bruin, a little less dignified, dropped on all fours, and walked leisurely off about ten rods; then raised again, jumped over a brush fence, and disappeared in the woods.

Next morning we looked for his tracks and, sure enough, there were the tracks of a large bear within four feet of the window. He had apparently stood and looked into the house.

The first Indian who troubled us was one by the name of John Williams. He was a large, powerful man, and certainly, very ugly. He used to pass our house and take our road to Dearbornville after fire-water, get a little drunk, and on his way back stop at John Blare's. Mr. Blare then lived at the end of our new road. Here the Indian would tell what great things he had done. One day when he stopped, Mrs. Blare and her brother-in-law, Asa, were there. He took a seat, took his knife from his belt, stuck it into the floor, then told Asa to pick it up and hand it to him; he repeated this action several times, and Asa obeyed him every time. He, seeing that the white man was afraid, said: "I have taken off the scalps of six damned Yankees with this knife and me take off one more."

When father heard this, with other things he had said, he thought he was the intended victim. We were all very much frightened. Whenever father was out mother was uneasy until his return, and he feared that the Indian, who always carried his rifle, might lay in ambush, and shoot him when he was at work.

One day he came along, as usual, from Dearbornville and passed our house. Father saw him, came in, took his rifle down from the hooks and told mother he believed he would shoot first. Mother would not hear a word to it and after living a year or two longer, in mortal fear of him, he died a natural death. We learned afterward that Joseph Pardee was the man he had intended to kill. He said, "Pardee had cut a bee-tree that belonged to Indian."

According to his previous calculation, on our arrival, father bought, in mother's name, eighty acres more, constituting the south-west quarter of section thirty-four, town two, south of range ten, east; bounded on the south by the south line of the town of Dearbon. A creek, we called the north branch of the River Ecorse, ran through it, going east. It was nearly parallel with, and forty-two rods from, the town line. When he entered it he took a duplicate; later his deed came, and it was signed by Andrew Jackson, a man whom father admired very much. Mother's deed came still later, signed by Martin Van Buren.

This land was very flat, and I thought, very beautiful. No waste land on it, all clay bottom, except about two acres, a sand ridge, resembling the side of a sugar loaf. This was near the centre of the place, and on it we finally built, as we found it very unpleasant living on clayey land in wet weather. This land was all heavy timbered—beech, hard maple, basswood, oak, hickory and some white-wood—on both sides of the creek; farther back, it was, mostly, ash and elm.

CHAPTER III.

HOW WE GOT OUR SWEET, AND THE HISTORY OF MY FIRST PIG.

We made troughs, tapped hard maples on each side of the creek; took our oxen, sled and two barrels (as the trees were scattered) to draw the sap to the place we had prepared for boiling it.

Now I had an employment entirely new to me: boiling down sap and making sugar, in the woods of Michigan. This was quite a help to us in getting along. We made our own "sweet" and vinegar, also some sugar and molasses to sell. Some springs, we made three or four hundred pounds of sugar. Sugar was not all the good things we had, for there was one added to my father's family, a little sister, who was none the less lovely, in my eye, because she was of Michigan, a native "Wolverine."

Now father's family, all told, consisted of mother and six children. The children grew to be men and women, and are all alive to this day, January 26, 1875.

After we came to Michigan mother's health constantly improved. She soon began to like her new home and became more cheerful and happy. I told her we had, what would be, a beautiful place; far better than the rocks and hills we left, I often renewed my promise that if she and I lived and I grew to be a man, we would go back, visit her friends and see again the land of her nativity.

To cheer her still more we received a letter from Mr. G. Purdy of York State, telling us that he was coming to Michigan in the fall, with his wife (mother's beloved sister, Abbie,) and her youngest sister, Sarah, was coming with them.

Asa Blare, the young man who picked up the Indian's knife, bought forty acres of government land joining us on the east, built him a house, went to Ohio, married and brought his wife back with him.

Now we had neighbors on the east of us, and Mr. Henry Travis (a brother-in-law of Mr. Pardee) came, bought land joining Mr. Pardee on the west, built and settled with a large family. About the same time many families from the East came and settled along the creek, for miles west of us.

Now we were on the border of civilization. Our next clearing of any importance was the little ridge. Father commenced around the edge, cut the brush and threw them from the ridge all around it to form a brush fence; then all the trees that would fall into the line of the fence were next felled, also, all that would fall over it, then those which would reach the fence were felled toward it. Then we trimmed them, cut the logs and piled the brush on the fence. I felt very much interested in clearing this piece. When father took his ax and started for work I took mine and was immediately at his side or a little behind him. In this manner we returned and we soon had the two acres cut off and surrounded by an immense log, tree-top and brush fence; at least, I thought it was a great fence. Now came the logging and burning, father worked with his oxen and handspike, I with my handspike. Some of the large logs near the fence he swung round with the oxen and left them by it. Others we drew together and when we piled them up, father took his handspike and rolled the log, I held it with mine until he got a new hold. In that way I helped him roll hundreds and thousands of logs. We soon had them all in heaps but they were green and burned slowly, some of them would not burn at all then. We scratched round them and put some seeds in every spot. We could do but very little with a plow. Father made a drag out of the crotch of a tree and put iron teeth in it; this did us some service as the land was exceedingly rooty.

In raising our summer crops we had to do most of the work with a hoe. Sometimes where it was very rooty we planted corn with an ax. In order to do this we struck the blade into the ground and roots about two inches, then dropped the corn in and struck again two or three inches from the first place which closed it and the hill of corn was planted.

Now I must go back to the first season and tell how I got my first pig. It was the first of the hog species we owned in Michigan. Father went to the village and I with him. From there we went down to Mr. Thompson's (the man who moved us out from Detroit). He wished father to see his hogs. They went to the yard, and as was my habit, I followed along. Mr. Thompson called the hogs up. I thought he had some very fine ones. Among them was an old sow that had some beautiful pigs. She seemed to be very cross, raised her bristles and growled at us, as much as to say, "Let my pigs alone."

I suppose Mr. Thompson thought he would have some sport with me, and being generous, he said: "If the boy will catch one I will give it to him." I selected one and started; I paid no attention to the old sow, but kept my eye on the pig I wanted, and the way I went for it was a caution. I caught it and ran for the fence, with the old sow after me. I got over very quickly and was safe with my pig in my arms. I started home; it kicked and squealed and tried to get away, but I held it tightly, patted it and called it "piggy." I said to myself, "'Now I have a pig of my own, it will soon grow up to be a hog, and we'll have pork." When I got home I put it in a barrel, covered it up so it could not get out and then took my ax, cut poles, and made it a new pen and put it on one place in Adam's world where pig and pig-pen had never been before. Now, thought I, I've got an ax, a pig and a gun.

One morning, a day or two after this, I went out and the pig was gone. Thinking it might have gone home, I went to Mr. Thompson's and enquired if they had seen it. I looked in the yard but the pig was not there. I made up my mind that it was lost, and started home. I followed the old trail, and when within sixty rods of the place where I now live, I met my pig. I was very glad to see it, but it turned from me and ran right into the woods. Now followed a chase which was very exciting to me. The pig seemed running for its life, I for my property, which was going off, over logs and through the brush, as fast as its legs could carry it. It was a hard chase, but I caught the pig and took it back. I made the pen stronger, and put it in again, but it would not eat much and in a few days after died, and away went all my imaginary pork.

Mr. Pardee had bought a piece of land for a Mr. Clapp, of Peakskill, New York, and was agent for the same. He said the south end of this land was openings. It was about one mile from our place, and Mr. Pardee offered to join with father and put corn on it, accordingly, we went to see it. There was some brush, but it was mostly covered with what we called "buffalo grass," which grew spontaneously. Cattle loved it very much in the summer, but their grazing it seemed to destroy it. It soon died out and mostly disappeared, scrub-oak and other brush coming up in its place.

Mr. Pardee and father soon cleared five or six acres of this land, and with the brush they cut made a light brush fence around it, then tore up three or four acres and planted it with corn. The soil was light yellow sand. When the corn came up it was small and yellow. They put in about two acres of buckwheat. A young man by the name of William Beal worked for Pardee. He helped to tend the corn. One morning, as they were going up to hoe the corn, William Beal took his gun and started ahead; this he frequently did very early. He said, when about half way to the corn, he looked toward the creek and saw a black bear coming toward him. He stood in the path, leading to the corn-field, which they had under-brushed. The bear did not discover him until he was near enough, when he fired and shot him dead. This raised quite an excitement among us. I went to see the bear. It was the first wild one I saw in Michigan. They dressed it, and so far as I know, the neighbors each had a piece; at all events, we had some.

They hoed the corn once or twice, and then made up their minds it was no use, as it would not amount to much, the land being too poor.

The whole crop of corn, gathered there, green at that, nubbins and all, was put into a half bushel handle basket, excepting what the squirrels took.

The buckwheat didn't amount to much, either. Wild turkeys trampled it down and ate the grain, in doing which, many of them lost their lives. I began to consider myself quite a marksman. I had already, with father's rifle, shot two deer, and had gotten some of the turkeys.

Father never cropped it any more on the openings, and his experience there made him much more pleased with his own farm. That land is near me, and I have seen a great many crops growing on it, both grain and other crops, but never one which I thought would pay the husbandman for his labor.

Father's partnership with Mr. Pardee was so unsuccessful on the openings, and in having to take the oxen back, and buy hay for them when that article was very high (their running out helped him some) that he concluded to go into partnership with Mr. Pardee, no more.

He sold half of his oxen to Asa Blare, who paid the money down, so their partnership opened in a little better shape. This partnership, father said, was necessary as our money had become very much reduced, and everything we bought, (such as flour and pork) was extremely dear; besides, we had no way to make a farthing except with our "maple-sweet" or the hide of a deer.

Father could not get work, for there were but few settlers, and none near him, who were able to hire. So he economized to save his money as much as possible, and worked at home. The clearing near the house grew larger and larger, and now we could see the beautiful sun earlier.

Father worked very hard, got three acres cleared and ready for wheat. Then he went away and bought about four bushels of white wheat for seed. This cost a snug sum in those days. About the last of August he sowed it and dragged it in with his drag. He sowed about a bushel and a peck to the acre. (I have for many years back, and to the present time, sowed two bushels to the acre).

His wheat came up and looked beautiful. The next spring and early summer it was very nice. One day a neighbor's unruly ox broke into it. I went through it to drive him out and it was knee high. Father said take the ox home. I did so. The neighbor was eating dinner. I told him his ox had been in our wheat and that father wished him to keep the ox away. He said we must make the fence better and he would not get in. This was the first unkind word I had received from a neighbor in Michigan. The wheat escaped the rust, headed and filled well and was an excellent crop. It helped us a great deal and was our manna in the wilderness.

Father and I continued our chopping until we connected the two clearings. Then we commenced to see the sun in the morning and we thought it shone brighter here than it did in York State. Some of the neighbors said that it really did, and that it might be on account of a reflection from the water of the great lakes. Perhaps it was because the deep gloom of the forest had shaded us so long and was now removed. Israel like, we looked back and longed for the good things we had left, viz:—apples, pears and the quince sauce. Even apples were luxuries we could not have and we greatly missed them. We cleared new ground, sowed turnip seed, dragged it in and raised some very large nice turnips. At this time there was not a wagon in the neighborhood, but Mr. Traverse, being a mechanic and ingenious, cut down a tree, sawed oft two short logs, used them for hubs and made the wheels for a cart. These he took to Dearbornville and had them ironed oft. He made the body himself and then had an ox-cart. This was the only wheeled vehicle in the place for some years. As Mr. Traverse was an obliging man the neighbors borrowed his cart. Sometimes it went to Dearbornville to bring in provision, or other things, and sometimes it went to mill. (There was a mill on the river Rouge, one mile north of Dearbornville.) With this cart and oxen the neighbors carried some of their first products, sugar, butter, eggs, &c., to Detroit. Some young sightseers, who had not seen Detroit since they moved into the woods and wished to see it, were on board. They had to start before midnight so it would be cool traveling for the oxen. This was the first cart and oxen ever seen in Detroit from our part of the town of Dearborn.

They reached home the following night, at about ten o'clock, and told me about the trip.

We wanted apples, so father took his oxen, went and borrowed the cart, loaded it with turnips, went down the river road half way to Detroit, traded them with a Frenchman for apples and brought home a load which were to us delicious fruit. In this way we got our apples for many years. These apples were small, not so large and nice as those we had been used to having; but they were Michigan apples and we appreciated them very much. They lasted us through the winter and did us much good.

CHAPTER IV.

OUR SECOND HOUSE AND
FIRST APPLE TREES.

Father said he would get us some apple trees. He had heard there was a small nursery below Dearbornville. One morning he and I started for the village; from there, we went to Mr. McVay's, about two miles east, near the Rouge.

Of him father bought thirteen apple trees, did them up in two bundles, his large, mine small. We took them on our shoulders and started home, through the woods, thus saving two miles travel. On our way we explored woods we had never seen before.

We planted the apple trees on the west end of the little ridge. They are now old trees. I passed them the other day and thought of the time we set them. Now some of them look as if they were dying with old age. I counted and found that some of them were gone. I thought there was no one but me, who could tell how, or when, those trees were planted, as they are nearly forty years old.

East of those trees father built his second house in 1836. He made the body of this house of large whitewood logs, split oak shakes with which to cover it, and dug a well east of the house. Into this well he put the shell of a large buttonwood log; we called it a "gum." It was said that water would not taste of buttonwood; we had very good water there.

Father borrowed Mr. Traverse's cart, loaded up our things and we were glad to leave our Bark Covered house, clay door-yard and Mr. Pardee's woods, to which we had lived so near, that we could see the sun only for a short time in the afternoon.

In the house we were leaving we had some unwelcome visitors, an Indian, John Williams, and a snake. One day, towards evening, mother was getting supper, and as the floor boards were lain down loosely they would shake as she walked across the floor. Some member of the family heard a strange noise (something rattling) which seemed to come from a chest that stood in the back part of the room on legs about six inches high. Every time mother stepped on the board upon which he was coiled up, his snakeship felt insulted and he would rattle to let them know that he was there and felt indignant at being disturbed. Mother said they all tried to find out what it was; they finally looked under the chest and there, to their astonishment, they saw a large black rattlesnake all curled up watching their movements and ready, with his poisonous fangs, to strike any one that came within his reach. He was an interloper, a little too bold. He had, however, gotten in the wrong place and was killed in the room. He had, no doubt, crawled up through a hole in the floor at the end of a board.

The children were very much alarmed and mother was frightened. She said she thought it was a terrible place where poisonous reptiles would crawl into the house. Near the house sometime after, brother John S. and sister Sarah were out raking up some scattering hay. I suppose sister was out for the sake of being out, or for her own amusement. While she was raking she saw a large blue racer close by her with his head up nearly as high as her own, looking at her and not seeming inclined to leave her. I never heard of a blue racer hurting any one and this was the only one I ever knew to make the attempt. Sister was greatly scared and hallooed and screamed, as if struck with terror. Brother John S., then a little way off ran to her as quickly as possible; while he was running the snake circled around her but a few feet off and seemed determined to attack her. Though brother was the younger of the two his courage was good. With the handle of his pitchfork he struck the snake across the back, a little below the head, and wounded him. Then he succeeded in sticking the tine of the pitchfork through the snake's head; at that sister Sarah took courage and tried with her rake to help brother in the combat. As she held up the handle the snake wound himself around it so tightly that he did not loosen his coils until he was dead. That snake measured between six and seven feet in length.

We knew nothing of this species of reptile until we came to Michigan. I have killed a great many of them, but have found that if one gets a rod or two the start, it is impossible to catch him. I well recollect having run after them across our clearing (where we first settled). They would go like a streak of blue, ahead. I make this statement of the reptiles, so that the people of Wayne County, or Michigan, who have no knowledge of such things may know something about the vexatious and fearful annoyances we had to contend with after we settled in Michigan.

We were all pleased when we got into the new house. We had a sand door-yard, and lived near the centre of our place. East of this house, on the little ridge, we raised our first patch of-water-melons, in Michigan. Father said they raised good melons on Long Island, where it was sandy soil, and he thought he could raise good ones there. He tried, and it proved to be a success; the melons were excellent. When they were ripe father borrowed the cart, picked a load of melons and (just before sundown) started for Detroit. Mother and my little Michigan sister, Abbie, went with us. I think it was the first time mother saw Detroit after she left it, on the morning following her first arrival there. She wished to do some trading, of course. Father and I walked. We took a little hay to feed the oxen on the road. The next morning we reached Detroit. The little market then stood near where the "Biddle House" now stands, or between that and the river.

Father sold his melons to a Frenchman for one shilling apiece. The market men said this was the first full load of melons ever on Detroit market; at all events, I know it was the first load of melons ever drawn from the town of Dearborn.

Mother's youngest sister lived in the city, and was at the store of Mr. Cook, or "Cook & Burns," where we did some of our trading. Their store was on Jefferson avenue. Mr. Cook was an eccentric man, and had his own way of recommending his goods, and one which made much sport. Auntie called for some calico. Mr. Cook took a piece off the shelf, threw it on the counter, threw up both arms, put his hands higher than his head, then picked it up again shook it and said: "There, who ever saw the like of that in Michigan? Two shillings a yard! A yard wide, foot thick and the colors as firm as the Allegheny Mountains!"

But an old colored woman came in who rather beat the clerk. She inquired for cheap calico; the clerk threw down some and told her the price. She said, "Oh that is too much! I want some cheap." Then the clerk threw down some that looked old and faded. With a broad grin, showing her teeth and the white of her eyes not a little, she said: "Oh, ho! my goot Lo'd dat war made when Jope war paby!"

When father and mother had traded all they could afford, it was nearly night, and we all got into the cart and started for home. We got upon the Chicago road opposite where the Grand Trunk Junction now is, and stopped. Mother thought she could not go any farther, and the oxen were tired. Father went into a log house on the north side of the Chicago road and asked them if they could keep us all night. They said they would, and we turned in. They used us first-rate, and treated us with much respect. Next morning after breakfast we went home.

CHAPTER V.

THE JUG OF WHISKY AND TEMPERANCE MEETING.

I have already said that, as money was getting short; father sold Asa Blare half of his oxen. They thought they could winter the oxen on marsh hay. They found some they thought very good on the creek bottom, about a mile and a quarter from where we lived. They said they would go right at work and cut it before some one else found it. As there was some water on the ground, and they would have to mow in the wet, they thought they would send and get a jug of whisky.

In the morning we had an early breakfast, and they ground up their scythes, then started, I with the jug, they with their scythes. We went together as far as our new road. Father told me after I got the whisky, to come back round the old trail to a certain place and call, when they heard me they would come and get the jug.

I went to Dearborn, got my jug filled, paid two shillings a gallon, or there-abouts, and started back. When I had gone as far as the turn of the road, where Dr. Snow now lives, out of sight, I thought to myself I'd take a drink. I had heard that whisky made one feel good and strong and as my jug was heavy, took what I called "a good horn;" I thought, however, it did not taste very pleasant. After that I went on as fast as I could, a little over a mile, till I got beyond where the road was cut out and into the trail, when I made up my mind I was stouter and my jug really seemed lighter. There I stopped again and took what I called "a good lifter." It burnt a little but I went on again till I came to the creek, then I called father who answered.

I felt so wonderfully good that I thought I'd take one more drink before he came in sight. So I took what I called "a good swig." When father came he said they had found plenty of good grass and he wished me to go and see it. I told him I didn't feel very well (I was afraid he would discover what I had been doing, I began to feel queer) but I followed along.

The grass was as high as my head in places and very heavy. It was what we call "blue-joint," mixed with a large coarse grass that grew three square at the butt. I got to the scythes where they had been mowing, told father I could mow that grass, took his scythe, cut a few clips and bent the blade very badly. (He often told afterwards, how much stronger I was than he, said he could mow the stoutest grass and not bend his scythe, but I had almost spoiled it.) I lay down the scythe, everything seemed to be bobbing up. I told father I was sick, he said I had better go home and I started gladly and as quickly as possible. The ground didn't seem to me to be entirely still, it wanted to raise up. I struck what I called a "bee-line" for home. When I got there I told mother I was sick, threw myself on her bed and kept as quiet as possible. When father came he inquired how I was; I heard what he said. Mother told him I was very sick but had got a little more quiet than I had been. He said they had better not disturb me so I occupied their bed all night, the first time I had ever had it all alone one night. The next morning I felt rather crest-fallen but congratulated myself in that they did not know what the trouble was, and they never knew (nor any of the rest of the family until I state it now). But I knew at the time what the trouble was, and the result was I had enough of whisky for many years, and took a decided stand for temperance.

Some years after that, there was a temperance meeting at a log school-house two miles and a half west of us. I was there and the house was full. After the opening speech, which pleased me very much, others were invited to speak. Thinking I must have a hand in I found myself on the floor. When I got there and commenced speaking, if it had been reasonable, I would have said I was somebody else, I would have been glad to have crawled out of some very small knot-hole, but I found it was I and that there was no escaping, so I proceeded.

Of course I did not relate my own experience, nor tell them that I had been sick. I gave them a little of the experience of others that I had heard. I had an old temperance song book from which I borrowed some extracts and appropriated them as my own. I swung my arms a little and with my finger pointed out the points. I stepped around a little and tried to stamp to make them believe that what I said was true. As I advanced and became more interested I spoke loud, to let them know it was I, and that I was in earnest. I admonished them all to let whisky alone. Told some of its pernicious effects; how much money it cost, how many lives it had taken, how many tears it had caused to flow and how many homes it had made desolate.

When I came away I was pleased with myself, and thought I had made quite a sensation. A few days afterward I met my friend, William Beal, and asked him how the neighbors liked the temperance meeting. Of course, I was anxious to know what they said about my speech. He told me the old lady said I was "fluent and tonguey," that I was like a sort of a lawyer, she named, who lived at Dearbornville. I knew this man well, and hadn't a very good opinion of him. But what she said was not so much of a breaker as what the old gentleman said, for I considered him in many respects a very intelligent man. He came here from Westchester County, near Peakskill. He owned the farm and lived on it (I have seen where he lived) which was given to John Spaulding for the capture of Major Andre. His occupation there was farming and droving. He drove cattle to New York city in an early day, when that great metropolis was but a small city. I have often heard him tell about stopping at Bullshead. He said that was the drovers' headquarters. I know he was worth ten thousand dollars there, at one time; how much more I cannot say, but somehow his thousands dwindled to hundreds and he came here to seek a second fortune.

Of course I thought a man of his experience was capable of forming a pretty correct opinion of me. He said, "Who is he? His father brought him here, and dropped him in the woods; he's been to mill once and to meeting twice. What does he know?"

When I heard this it amused me very much, although the decision seemed to be against me. I made no more inquiries about temperance meeting, in fact, I didn't care to hear any more about it.

Writing my first temperance effort has blown all the wind out of my sails, and if I were not relating actual occurrences I should certainly be run ashore. As it is, sleep may invigorate and bring back my memory. When relating facts it is not necessary to call on any muse, or fast, or roam into a shady bower, where so many have found their thoughts. When relating facts, fancy is hot required to soar untrodden heights where thought has seldom reached; but too freely come back all the weary days, the toils, fears and vexations of my early life in Michigan, if not frightened away by the memory of the decision of the old lady and gentleman, on my temperance speech.

Perhaps I should say, in honor of that old gentleman, Mr. Joseph Pardee, now deceased, that he was well advanced in years when he came to Michigan, in the fall of 1833, stuck his stakes and built the first log house on the Ecorse, west of the French settlement, at its mouth, on Detroit River. He was a man of a strong-mind and an iron will. He cleared up his land, made it a beautiful farm, rescued it from the wilderness, acquired, in fact, a good fortune. When he died, at the good old age of eighty-one years, he left his family in excellent circumstances. He died in the year one thousand eight hundred and fifty-nine.

CHAPTER VI.

HOW WE FOUND OUR CATTLE.

The old cow always wore the bell. Early in the spring, when there were no flies or mosquitoes to drive them up the cattle sometimes wandered off. At such times, when we went to our chopping or work, we watched them, to see which way they went, and listened to the bell after they were out of sight in order that we might know which way to go after them if they didn't return. Sometimes the bell went out of hearing but I was careful to remember which way I heard it last.

Before night I would start to look for them, going in the direction I last heard them. I would go half a mile or so into the woods, then stop and listen, to see if I could hear the faintest sound of the bell. If I could not hear it I went farther in the same direction then stopped and listened again. Then if I did not hear it I took another direction, went a piece and stopped again, and if I heard the least sound of it I knew it from all other bells because I had heard it so often before.

That bell is laid up with care. I am now over fifty years old, but if the least tinkling of that bell should reach my ear I should know the sound as well as I did when I was a boy listening for it in the woods of Michigan.

When I found the cattle I would pick up a stick and throw it at them, halloo very loudly and they would start straight for home. Sometimes, in cloudy weather, I was lost and it looked to me as though they were going the wrong way, but I followed them, through black-ash swales where the water was knee-deep, sometimes nearly barefooted.

I always carried a gun, sometimes father's rifle. The deer didn't seem to be afraid of the cattle; they would stand and look at them as they passed not seeming to notice me. I would walk carefully, get behind a tree, and take pains to get a fair shot at one. When I had killed it I bent bushes and broke them partly off, every few rods, until I knew I could find the place again, then father and I would go and get the deer.

Driving the cattle home in this way I traveled hundreds of miles. There was some danger then, in going barefooted as there were some massassauga all through the woods. As the country got cleared up they disappeared, and as there are neither rocks, ledges nor logs, under which they can hide, I have not seen one in many years.

One time the cattle strayed off and went so far I could not find them. I looked for them until nearly dark but had to return without them. I told father where I had been and that I could not hear the bell. The next morning father and I started to see if we could find them. We looked two or three days but could not find or hear anything of them. We began to think they were lost in the wilderness. However, we concluded to look one more day, so we started and went four or five miles southeast until we struck the Reed creek. (Always known as the Reed creek by us for the reason, a man by the name of Reed came with his family from the State of New York, built him a log house and lived there one summer. His family got sick, he became discouraged, and in the fall moved back to the State of New York. The place where he lived, the one summer, was about two miles south of our house and this creek is really the middle branch of the Ecorse).

There was no settlement between us and the Detroit River, a distance of six miles. We looked along the Reed creek to see if any cattle had crossed it.

While we were looking there we heard the report of a rifle close by us and hurried up. It was an Indian who had just shot a duck in the head. When we came to him father told him it was a lucky shot, a good shot to shoot it in the head. He said, "Me allers shoot head not hurt body." He took us to his wigwam, which was close by, showed us another duck with the neck nearly shot off. Whether he told the truth, or whether these two were lucky shots, I cannot tell, but one thing I do know, in regard to him, if he told us the truth he was an extraordinary man and marksman.

Around his wigwam hung from half a dozen to a dozen deer skins; they hung on poles. His family seemed to consist of his squaw and a young squaw almost grown up. Father told him we had lost our cattle, oxen and cow, and asked him if he had seen them. We had hard work to make him understand what we meant. Father said—cow—bell—strap round neck—he tried to show him, shook his hand as if jingling a bell. Then father said, oxen—spotted—white—black; he put his hand on his side and said: black—cow—bell—noise, and then said, as nearly as we could understand, "Me see them day before yesterday," and he pointed in the woods to tell us which way. Father took a silver half-dollar out of his pocket, showed it to the Indian, and told him he should have it if he would show us the cattle. He wiped out his rifle, loaded it and said, "Me show." He took his rifle and wiper and started with us; we went about half a mile and he showed us where he had seen them. We looked and found large ox's tracks and cow's tracks. I thought, from the size and shape of them, they were our cattle's tracks. The Indian started upon the tracks, father followed him, and I followed father. When we came to high ground, where I could hardly see a track; the Indian had no trouble in following them, and he went on a trot. I had hard work to keep up with him. I remember well how he looked, with his bowing legs, it seemed as if he were on springs. He moved like an antelope, with such ease and agility. He looked as if he hardly touched the ground.

The cattle, in feeding round, crossed their own tracks sometimes. The Indian always knew which were the last tracks. He followed all their crooks, we followed him by sight, which gave us a little the advantage, and helped us to keep in sight. He led us, crooking about in this way, for nearly two hours, when we came in hearing of the bell. I never had a harder time in the woods but once, and it was when I was older, stronger, and better able to stand a chase, that time I was following four bears, and an Indian tried to get them away. I was pleased when we got to the cattle. Father paid the Indian the half-dollar he had earned so well, and thanked him most heartily, whether he understood it or not. Father asked the Indian the way home, he said, "My house, my wigwam, which way my home?" The Indian pointed with his wiper, and showed us the way.

Father said afterward, it was strange that the Indian should know where he lived, as he had never seen him before. I never saw that Indian afterward.

The cattle were feeding on cow-slips and leeks, which grew in abundance, also on little French bogs that had just started up. We hallooed at them very sharply and they started homeward, we followed them, and that night found our cattle home again. Mother and all the children were happy to see them come, for they were our main dependence. They were called many dear names and told not to go off so far any more.

CHAPTER VII.

TROUBLE CAME ON THE WING.

Among the annoyances common to man and beast in Michigan, of which we knew nothing where we came from, were some enormous flies. There were two kinds that were terrible pests to the cattle. They actually ate the hide off, in spots. First we put turpentine, mixed with sufficient grease so as not to take the hair off, on those spots. But we found that fish oil was better, the flies would not bite where that was.

What we called the ox-flies were the most troublesome. In hot weather and in the sun, where the mosquitoes didn't trouble, they were most numerous. They would light on the oxen in swarms, on their brisket, and between their legs where they could not drive them off. I have frequently struck these flies with my hand and by killing them got my hand red with the blood of the ox.

The other species of flies, we called Pontiacers. This is a Michigan name, and originated I was told, from one being caught near Pontiac with a paper tied or attached to it having the word Pontiac written upon it.

These flies were not very numerous; sometimes there were three or four around at once. When they were coming we could hear and see them for some rods. Their fashion was to circle around the oxen before lighting on them. I frequently slapped them to kill them, sometimes I caught them, in that case they were apt to lose their heads, proboscis and all. These flies were very large, some were black and some of the largest were whitish on the front of the back. I have seen some of them nearly as large as young humming birds. The Germans tell me they have this kind of fly in Germany. But with the mosquitoes, these flies have nearly disappeared.

CHAPTER VIII.

HARD TIMES FOR US IN MICHIGAN, 1836-7.

The oxen having worked hard and been used to good hay, which we bought for them, grew poor when they were fed on marsh hay. Then Mr. Blare wanted to sell his part to father; then the cattle would not have so much to do. Father was not able to buy them, as his money was nearly gone. He said he would mortgage his lot for one hundred dollars, buy them back, buy another cow and have a little money to use.

He said he could do his spring's work with the cattle, then turn them off, fatten them, and sell them in the fall for enough to pay the mortgage. Mother said all she could to prevent it, for she could not bear the idea of having her home mortgaged. It seemed actually awful to me, for I thought we should not be able to pay it, and in all probability we should lose the place. I said all I could, but to no avail. The whole family was alarmed; one of the small children asked mother what a mortgage was, she replied that it was something that would take our home away from us, if not paid.

Father went to Dearbornville and mortgaged his lot to Mrs. Phlihaven, a widow woman, for one hundred dollars, said to be at seven per cent., as that was lawful interest then. We supposed, at the time, he got a hundred dollars, but he got only eighty. Probably the reason he did not let us know the hard conditions of the mortgage, was because we opposed it so. Mrs. Phlihaven said as long as he would pay the twenty dollars shave money, and the seven dollars interest annually, she would let it run. And it did run until the shave money and interest more than ate up the principal.

Father bought the oxen back for the old price, forty dollars, and bought another cow, of Mr. McVay, for which he paid eighteen dollars, leaving him twenty-two dollars of the hired money.

It was now spring, the oxen became very poor, one of them was taken sick and got down. Father said he had the hollow horn and doctored him for that; but I think to day, if the oxen had had a little corn meal, and good hay through the winter, they would have been all right.

After the ox got down, and we could not get him up he still ate and seemed to have a good appetite. I went to Dearbornville, bought hay at the tavern and paid at the rate of a dollar a hundred. I tied it up in a rope, carried it home on my back and fed it to him. Then I went into the woods, with some of the other children, and gathered small brakes that lay flat on the ground. They grew on beech and maple land, and kept green all winter. The ox ate some of them, but he died; our new cow, also, died in less than two weeks after father bought her. Then we had one ox, our old cow, and two young cattle we had raised from her, that we kept through the spring. In the summer the other ox had the bloody murrain and he died.

Then we had no team, no money to get a team with, and our place was mortgaged. Now when father got anything for the family he had to bring it home himself. We got out of potatoes, these he bought at Dearbornville, paid a dollar a bushel for them, and brought them home on his back. He sent me to the village for meal. I called for it and the grocerman measured it to me in a quart measure which was little at the top, such as liquors are measured with. I carried the meal home. In this way we had to pack home everything we bought.

When potatoes got ripe we had plenty of the best. On father's first visit to Michigan he was told that the soil of Michigan would not produce good potatoes. We soon found that this was a mistake for we had raised some good ones before, but not enough to last through the summer.

We still had wheat but sometimes had to almost do without groceries. We always had something to eat but sometimes our living was very poor. Sometimes we had potatoes and milk and sometimes thickened milk. This was made by dampening flour, rolling it into fine lumps and putting them into boiling milk with a little salt, and stirring it until it boiled again. This was much more palatable than potatoes and milk.

One afternoon two neighbors' girls came to visit us. They stayed late. After they went away I asked mother why she didn't give them some tea; she said she had no tea to give them, and that if she had given them the best she had they would have gone away and told how poor we were.

Mother had been used to better days and to treating her guests well, and her early life in Michigan did not take all of her spirit away. She was a little proud as well as I, but I have learned that pride, hard times and poverty are very poor companions. It was no consolation to think that the neighbors, most of them, were as bad off as we were. This made the thing still worse.

CHAPTER IX.

A SUMMER HUNT.

Father and I went hunting one day. I took my shot-gun, loaded with half a charge of shot and three rifle bullets, which just chambered in the barrel, so I thought I was ready to shoot at anything. Father went ahead and I followed him; we walked very carefully in the woods looking for deer; went upon a sand ridge where father saw a deer and shot at it. I recollect well how it looked; it was a beautiful deer, almost as red as a cherry. After he shot, it stood still. I asked father, in a whisper, if I might not shoot. He said, "Keep still!" (I had very hard word to do so, and think if he had let me shot, I should have given it a very loud call, at least, I think I should have killed it.) Father loaded his rifle and shot again. The last time he shot, the deer ran away. We went to the place where it had stood. He had hit it for we found a little blood; but it got away.

It is said "the leopard cannot change his spots nor the Ethiopian his skin," but the deer, assisted by nature, can change both his color and his hide. In summer the deer is red, and the young deer are covered with beautiful spots which disappear by fall. The hair of the deer is short in summer and his hide is thick. At this time the hide is most valuable by the pound. His horns grow and form their prongs, when growing we call them in their velvet; feel of them and they are soft, through the summer and fall, and they keep growing until they form a perfect horn, hard as a bone. By the prongs we are able to tell the number of years old they are.

In the fall of the year when an old buck has his horns fully grown to see him running in his native forest is a beautiful sight. At that season his color has changed to a bluish grey. When the weather gets cold and it freezes hard his horns drop off, and he has to go bareheaded until spring. Then his hair is very long and grey. Deer are commonly poor in the spring, and at this season their hide is very thin and not worth much. So we see the deer is a very singular animal. As I have been going through the woods I have often picked up their horns and carried them home for curiosities. They were valuable for knife-handles.

When the old buck is started from his bed and is frightened how he clears the ground. You can mark him from twenty to thirty feet at every jump. (I have measured some of his jumps, by pacing, and found them to be very long, sometimes two rods.) How plump he is, how symmetrically his body is formed, and how beautiful the appearance of his towering, branching antlers! As he carries them on his lofty head they appear like a rocking chair. As he sails through the air, with his flag hoisted, he sometimes gives two or three of his whistling snorts and bids defiance to all pursuers in the flight. He is able to run away from any of his enemies, in a fair foot race, but not always able to escape from flying missiles of death.

Before the fawn is a year old, if frightened and startled from its bed, it runs very differently from the old deer. Its jump is long and high. It appears as though it were going to jump up among the small tree tops. The next jump is short and sometimes sidewise, then another long jump and so on. It acts as though it did not know its own springs, or were cutting up its antics, and yet it always manages to keep up with the rest of the deer.

Father had killed some deer. He shot one of the largest red bucks I had seen killed. After this we wanted meat. Father said we'll go hunting and see if we can get a deer. He said I might take his rifle and he would take my gun. (For some reason or other he had promoted me, may be he thought I was luckier than he.) We started out into the woods south of our house, I went ahead. There was snow on the ground, it was cold and the wind blew very hard. We crossed the windfall. This was a strip of land about eighty rods wide. It must have been a revolving whirlwind that past there, for it had taken down pretty much all the timber and laid it every way. Nothing was left standing except some large trees that had little tops, these were scattered here and there through the strip. It struck the southeast corner of what was afterward our place. Here we had about three acres of saplings, brush and old logs that were windfalls.

I think this streak of wind must have passed about ten years before we came to the country. It came from the openings in the town of Taylor, went a northeast course until it struck the Rouge (after that I have no knowledge of it.) In this windfall had grown up a second growth of timber, saplings and brush, so thick that it was hard work to get through or see a deer any distance. We got south of the windfall and scared up a drove of deer, some four or five.

The woods were cracking and snapping all around us; we thought it was dangerous and were afraid to be in the woods. Still we thought we would run the risk and follow the deer. They ran but a little ways, stopped and waited until we came in sight, then ran a little ways again. They seemed afraid to run ahead and huddled up together, the terrible noise in the timber seemed to frighten them. The last time I got sight of them they were in a small opening standing by some large old logs. I remember well to this day just how the place looked. I drew up the rifle and shot. Father was right behind me; I told him they didn't run. He took the rifle and handed me my gun, saying, "Shoot this." I shot again, this gun was heavily loaded and must have made a loud report, but could not have been heard at any great distance on account of the roaring wind in the tree-tops. The deer were still in sight, I took the rifle, loaded it, and shot again; then we loaded both guns but by this time the deer had disappeared. We went up to where they had stood and there lay a beautiful deer. Then we looked at the tracks where the others had run off, and found that one went alone and left a bloody trail, but we thought best to leave it and take home the one we had killed. When we got home we showed our folks what a fat heavy deer we had and they were very much pleased, as this was to be our meat in the wilderness.

A man by the name of Wilson was at our house and in the afternoon he volunteered to go with us after the other deer. We took our dog and started taking our back tracks to where we left; we followed the deer but a very little ways before we came across the other one we had hit; it had died, and we took it home, thinking we had been very fortunate. Here I learned that deer could be approached in a windy time better than in any other. I also learned that the Almighty, in His wisdom, provided for his creatures, and caused the elements, wind and snow, to work together for their good.

Now we were supplied with meat for a month, with good fat venison, not with quails, as God supplied his ancient people over three thousand years before, in the wilderness of Sinai, or at the Tabernacle, where six hundred thousand men wept for flesh, and there went forth a wind and brought quails from the Red Sea. No doubt they were fat and delicious, and the wind let them fall by the camp, and around about the camp, for some distance. They were easily caught by hungry men. Thus was the wind freighted with flesh to feed that peculiar people a whole month and more.

When the terrific wind, that helped us to capture the deer, raged through the tree-tops it sounded like distant thunder. It bent the tall trees, in unison, all one way, as if they agreed to bow together before the power that was upon them. When they straightened up they shook their tops as though angry at one another, broke off some of the limbs which they had borne for years, and sent them crashing to the ground.

Some of the trees were blown up by the roots, and if allowed to remain would in time form such little mounds as we children took to be Indian graves when we first came into the woods. Those little mounds are monuments, which mark the places where some of those ancient members of the forest stood centuries ago, and they will remain through future ages unless obliterated by the hand of man.

We thought that the wind blew harder here than in York State, where we came from. We supposed the reason was that the mountains and hills of New York broke the wind off, and this being a flat country with nothing to break the force of the wind, except the woods, we felt it more severely.

CHAPTER X.

HOW WE GOT INTO TROUBLE ONE NIGHT, AND I SCARED.

One warm day in winter father and I went hunting. I had the rifle that day. We went south, crossed the windfall and Reed creek, and went into what we called the "big woods." We followed deer, but seemed to be very unlucky, for I couldn't shoot them. We travelled in the woods all day and hunted the best we could.

Just at sundown, deer that have been followed all day are apt to stop and browse a little. Then if the wind is favorable and blowing from them to you, it is possible to get a shot at them; but if the wind is blowing from you to them, you can't get within gunshot of them. They will scent you. They happened to be on the windward side, as we called it. I got a shot at one and killed it. It was late and, carelessly, I didn't load the rifle. It being near night, I thought I should not have a chance to shoot anything more.

It was my custom to load the rifle after shooting, and if I didn't have any use for it before, when I got near home, I shot at a mark on a tree or something. In that way I practiced shooting and let the folks know I was coming. In this way I also kept the rifle from rusting, as sometimes it was wet; when I got into the house I cleaned it off and wiped it out.

In a few minutes we had skinned the two fore quarters out. Then we wrapped the fore part of the hide around the hind quarters, and each took a half and started. It was now dark, and we did not like to undertake going home straight through the woods, so took our way to the Reed house, from which there was a dim path through to Pardee's, and we could find our way home.

We were tired and hungry, and our feet were wet from travelling through the soft snow. As Mr. Reed had moved away there was no one in the house, and we went in and kindled a fire in the fireplace. The way we did it, I took some "punk" wood out of my pocket, held flint stone over it, struck the flint with my knife, and the punk soon took fire. We put a few whitlings on it, then some sticks we had gathered in the way near by the house. We soon had a good fire and were warming and drying our feet.

This "punk" I got from soft maple trees. When I wanted some I went into the woods and looked for an oldish tree, looked up, and if I could see black knots on the body of the tree, toward the top, I knew there was "punk" wood in it and would cut it down, then cut half way through the log, above and below the black knot, and split it off. In the center of the log I was sure to find "punk" wood. Sometimes, in this way, I got enough to last a year or two from one tree. It was of a brown color and was found in layers, which were attached and adhered together. When I chopped a tree I took out all I could find, carried it home, laid it up in a place where it would get drier, and it was always ready for use.

We had to use the utmost precaution not to get out of this material. Sometimes I have known my little Michigan sister, Abbie, to go more than a quarter of a mile, to the Blare place, to borrow fire; on such occasions we had to wait for breakfast until she returned. I do not know that the fire was ever paid back, but I do know that we had callers frequently when the errand was to borrow fire.

When I went hunting I was careful to take a piece of this with me. I broke or tore it off (it was something like tearing old cloth). With this, a flint and a jackknife I could make a fire in case night overtook me in the woods and I could not get out. Fire was our greatest protection from wild animals and cold in the night. This was the way we kindled our fire in the Reed house, before "Lucifer matches" or "Telegraph matches" were heard of by us, although they were invented as early as 1833. After we got a little comfortable and rested, and the wood burned down to coals we cut some slices of venison, laid them on the coals and roasted them. Although we had no salt, the meat tasted very good.

Late in the evening we took our venison and started again. It was hard work to follow the path in the thick woods, and we had to feel the way with our feet mostly as it was quite dark. We had got about eighty rods from the house when, as unexpected as thunder in the winter, broke upon our startled ears the dismal yells and awful howls of wolves. No doubt they had smelled our venison and come down from the west, came down almost upon us and broke out with their hideous yells. The woods seemed to be alive with them. Father said: "Load the rifle quick!" I dropped my venison, and if ever I loaded a gun quick, in the dark, it was then. I threw in the powder, ran down a ball without a patch, and, strange to say, before I got the cap on the wolves were gone, or at least they were still, we didn't even hear them run or trot. What it was that frightened them we never knew; whether it was our stopping so boldly or the smell of the powder, or what, I cannot say; but we did refuse to let them have our venison. We got away with it as quickly as possible and carried it safety home.

Another wolf adventure worth relating: I had been deer hunting; I had been off beyond what we called the Indian hill and was returning home. I was southwest of this hill, and on the north side of a little ridge which ran to the hill, when two wolves came from the south. They ran over the little ridge, crossing right in front of me, to go into a big thicket north. I had my rifle on them. They did halt, but in shooting very quickly I did not get a very good sight, however, I knocked one down and thought I had killed him. (They were just about of a size, and when I shot, the other went back like a flash the way he came from.) I loaded the rifle, but before I had it loaded the one I had shot got up and looked at me. I saw what I had done. I had cut off his lower jaw, close up, and it hung down. Another shot finished him quickly. He measured six feet from the end of his nose to the point of his tail.

I have seen many wolves, I have seen them in shows, but never saw any that compared in size with these Michigan wolves. It takes a very large, long dog to measure five feet. There was a bounty on wolves. I went down through the woods to Squire Goodel's, who lived near the Detroit river, got him to make out my papers and got the bounty. These pests were more shy in the day-time. They were harder to get a shot at than the deer. There were many of them in the woods, and we heard them so often nights that we became familiar with them. When the "Michigan Central Railroad" was built, and the cars ran through Dearborn, there was something about the iron track, or the noise of the cars which drove them from the country.

CHAPTER XI.

THE INDIANS VISIT US—
THEIR STRANGE AND PECULIAR WAYS.

Some three or four years after we came to the country there came a tribe, or part of a tribe, of Indians and camped a little over a mile southwest of our house, in the timber, near the head of the windfall next to the openings. They somewhat alarmed us, but father said, "Use them well, be kind to them and they will not harm us." I suppose they came to hunt. It was in the summer time and the first we knew of them, my little brother and two sisters had been on the openings picking huckleberries not thinking of Indians. When they started home and got into the edge of the woods they were in plain sight of Indians, and they said it appeared as if the woods were full of them. They stood for a minute and saw that the Indians were peeling bark and making wigwams: they had some trees already peeled.

They said they saw one Indian who had on a sort of crown, or wreath, with feathers in it that waved a foot above his head. They saw him mount a sorrel pony. As he did so the other Indians whooped and hooted, I suppose to cheer the chief. Childlike they were scared and thought that he was coming after them on horseback. They left the path and ran right into the brush and woods, from home. When they thought they were out of sight of the Indian they turned toward home. After they came in sight of home, to encourage his sisters, my little brother told them, he wouldn't be afraid of any one Indian but, he said, there were so many there it was enough to scare anybody. When they got within twenty rods of the house they saw some one coming beyond the house with a gun on his shoulder. One said it was William Beal, another said it was an Indian. They looked again and all agreed that it was an Indian. If they had come straight down the lane, they would have just about met him at the bars, opposite the house, (where we went through). There was no way for them to get to the house and shun him; except to climb the fence and run across the field. The dreaded Indian seemed to meet them everywhere, and if possible they were more scared now than before. Brother and sister Sarah were over the fence very quickly. Bessie had run so hard to get home and was so scared that in attempting to climb the fence she got part way up and fell back, but up and tried again. Sister Sarah would not leave her but helped her over. But John S. left them and ran for his life to the house; as soon as they could get started they ran too. Mother said Smith ran into the house looking very scared, and went for the gun. She asked him what was the matter, and what he wanted of the gun; he said there was an Indian coming to kill them and he wanted to shoot him. Mother told him to let the gun alone, the Indian would not hurt them; by this time my sisters had got in. In a minute or two afterward the Indian came in, little thinking how near he had come being shot by a youthful hero.

Poor Indian wanted to borrow a large brass kettle that mother had and leave his rifle as security for it. Mother lent him the kettle and he went away. In a few days he brought the kettle home.

A short time after this a number of them had been out to Dearbornville and got some whisky. All but one had imbibed rather too freely of "Whiteman's fire water to make Indian feel good." They came down as far as our house and, as we had no stick standing across the door, they walked in very quietly, without knocking. The practice or law among the Indians is, when one goes away from his wigwam, if he puts a stick across the entrance all are forbidden to enter there; and, as it is the only protection of his wigwam, no Indian honorably violates it. There were ten of these Indians. Mother was washing. She said the children were very much afraid, not having gotten over their fright. They got around behind her and the washtub, as though she could protect them. The Indians asked for bread and milk; mother gave them all she had. They got upon the floor, took hold of hands and formed a ring. The sober one sat in the middle; the others seemed to hear to what he said as much as though he had been an officer. He would not drink a drop of the whisky, but kept perfectly sober. They seemed to have a very joyful time, they danced and sang their wild songs of the forest. Then asked mother for more bread and milk; she told them she had no more; then they asked for buttermilk and she gave them what she had of that. As mother was afraid, she gave them anything she had, that they called for. They asked her for whisky; she said she hadn't got it. They said, "Maybe you lie." Then they pointed toward Mr. Pardee's and said, "Neighbor got whisky?" She told them she didn't know. They said again, "Maybe you lie."

When they were ready the sober one said, "Indian go!" He had them all start in single file. In that way they went out of sight. Mother was overjoyed and much relieved when they were gone. They had eaten up all her bread and used up all her milk, but I suppose they thought they had had a good time.

Not more than two or three weeks after this the Indians moved away, and these children of the forest wandered to other hunting grounds. We were very much pleased, as well as the other neighbors, when they were gone.

Father had a good opinion of the Indians, though he had been frightened by the first one, John Williams, and was afraid of losing his life by him. He considered him an exception, a wicked, ugly Indian. Thought, perhaps, he had been driven away from his own tribe, and was like Cain, a vagabond upon the face of the earth. He was different from other Indians, as some of them had the most sensitive emotions of humanity. If you did them a kindness they would never forget it, and they never would betray a friend; but if you offended them or did them an injury, they would never forget that either. These two traits of character run parallel with their lives and only terminate with their existence.

I recollect father's relating a circumstance that happened in the State of New York, about the time of the Revolutionary War. He said an Indian went into a tavern and asked the landlord if he would give him something to eat. The landlord repulsed him with scorn, told him he wouldn't give him anything and to get out of the house, for he didn't want a dirty Indian around. There was a gentleman sitting in the room who saw the Indian come in and heard what was said. The Indian started to go; the gentleman stepped up and said: "Call him back, give him what he wants, and I'll pay for it." The Indian went back, had a good meal and was well used; then he went on his way and the gentleman saw him no more, at that time.

Shortly after this the gentleman emigrated to the West, and was one of the advanced guards of civilization. He went into the woods, built him a house and cleared a piece of land. About this time there was a war in the country. He was taken captive and carried away a long distance, to an Indian settlement. He was tried, by them, for his life, condemned to death and was to be executed the next morning. He was securely bound and fastened. The chief detailed an Indian who, he thought, knew something of the whites and their tricks and would be capable of guarding the captive safely, and he was set as a watch to keep him secure until morning. I have forgotten what father said was to have been the manner of his execution; whether he was to be tomahawked or burned, at all events he was to meet his fate in the morning. Late in the night, after the warriors were fast asleep and, perhaps, dreaming of their spoils, when everything was still in the camp, the Indian untied and loosed the captive, told him to be careful, still, and follow him. After they were outside the camp, out of hearing, the Indian told the white man that he was going to save his life and show him the way home. They traveled until morning and all that day, and the night following, the next morning they came out in sight of a clearing and the Indian showed him a house and asked him if he knew the place; he said he did. Then the Indian asked him if he knew him; he told him that he did not. Then he referred him to the tavern and asked if he remembered giving an Indian something to eat. He said he did. "I am the one," said the Indian, "and I dare not go back to my own tribe, they would kill me." Here the friends par Led to meet no more. One went home to friends and civilization; the other went an exile without friends to whom he dared go, with no home, a fugitive in the wilderness.

There was a man by the name of H. Moody who often visited at father's house he told me that when he was young he was among the Mohawk Indians in Canada. This tribe formerly lived in what is now the State of New York. They took up on the side of the English, were driven away to Canada and there settled on the Grand River. Mr. Moody was well acquainted with the sons of the great chief, Brant, and knew the laws and customs of the tribe. He said when they considered one of their tribe very bad they set him aside and would have nothing to do with him.

If one murdered another of the same tribe he was taken up and tried by a council, and if it was found to be wilful murder, without any cause, he was condemned and put to death; but if there were any extenuating circumstances which showed that he had some reason for it, he was condemned and sentenced, by the chief, to sit on the grave of his victim for a certain length of time. That was his only hope and his "City of refuge." If any of the relatives of the deceased wanted to kill him there they had a right (according to their law) to do so. If he remained and lived his time out, on the horrible place, he was received back again to the fellowship of his tribe. This must have been a terrible punishment. It showed, however, the Indian's love of his tribe and country, to sit there and think of the danger of being shot or tomahawked, and of the terrible deed he had committed. He had taken away what he could never give. How different was his case from the one who left tribe, friends and home, and ran away to save the life of a white man who had given him bread.

About two and a half miles southwest of our house there was a large sand hill. Huckleberries grew there in abundance. I went there and picked some myself. On the top of that hill we found Indian graves, where some had been recently buried. There were pens built of old logs and poles around them, and we called it the "Indian Hill." It is known by that name to this day. The old telegraph road runs right round under the brow of this hill. This hill is in the town of Taylor. I don't suppose there are many in that town who do not know the hill or have heard of it, and but few in the town of Dearborn. I don't suppose there are six persons living who know the reason it is called the "Indian Hill" for we named it in a very early day.

Some twelve or fifteen years after this a man by the name of Clark had the job of grading down a sand hill nearly a mile south of Taylor Center. In grading he had to cut down the bank six or seven feet and draw it off on to the road. He hired me with my team to go and help him. I went. He had been at work there before and he showed me some Indian bones that he had dug up and laid in a heap. He said that two persons were buried there. From the bones, one must have been very large, and the other smaller. He had been very careful to gather them up. He said he thought they were buried in a sitting or reclining posture, as he came to the skulls first. The skulls, arm and thigh bones were in the best state of preservation, and in fact, the most that was left of them.

I took one thigh bone that was whole, sat down on the bank and we compared it with my own. As I was six feet, an inch and a half, we tried to measure the best we could to learn the size of the Indian. We made up our minds that he was at least seven, or seven and a half, feet tall. I think it likely it was his squaw who sat by his side. They must have been buried a very long time. We dug a hole on the north side of a little black oak tree that stood on the hill west of the road, and there we deposited all that remained of those ancient people. I was along there the other day (1875) and as I passed I noticed the oak. It is now quite a large tree; I thought there was no one living in this country, but me, who knew what was beneath its roots. No doubt that Indian was a hunter and a warrior in his day. He might have heard, and been alarmed, that the white man had come in big canoes over the great waters and that they were stopping to live beyond the mountains. But little did he think that in a few moons, or "skeezicks" as they called it, he should pass to the happy hunting ground, and his bones be dug up by the white man, and hundreds and thousands pass over the place, not knowing that once a native American and his squaw were buried there. That Indian might have sung this sentiment:

> "And when this life shall end,
>   When calls the great So-wan-na,
> Southwestern shall I wend,
>   To roam the great Savannah."
>
> —*Bishop*,

No doubt he was an observer of nature. In his day he had listened to the voice of Gitche Manito, or the Great Spirit, in the thunder and witnessed the display of his power in the lightning, as it destroyed the monster oak and tore it in slivers from top to bottom, and the voice of the wind, all told him that there was a Great Spirit. It told him if Indian was good he would go to a better place, where game would be plenty, and, no one would drive him away. No doubt he had made preparation for his departure and wanted his bow, arrow, and maybe other things, buried with him. If this was so they had disappeared as we found nothing of the kind. It is known to be the belief of the Indian in his wild state, that he will need his bow and arrow, or his gun and powder horn, or whatever he has to hunt with here, to use after lie has passed over to the happy hunting ground.

About the time that Clark dug up the bones, I became acquainted with something that I never could account for and it has always been a mystery to me. An Englishman was digging a ditch on the creek bottom, to drain the creek, a little over three-quarters of a mile west of father's house. He was digging it six feet wide and two feet deep, where brush called grey willows stood so thick that it was impossible for a man to walk through them. He cut the brush and had dug eight or ten inches when he came to red earth. Some day there had been a great fire at this place. The streak of red ground was about an inch thick, and in it he found what all called human bones. I went to see it myself and the bones we gathered up were mostly small pieces, no whole ones; but we saw enough to convince us that they were human bones. The ground that was burned over might have been, from the appearance, twelve feet square. It must have been done a great many years before, for the ground to make, and the brush to grow over it.

This creek, the Ecorse, not being fed by any rivulets or springs from hills or mountains, is supplied entirely by surface water. It is sometimes quite a large stream, but during dry weather in the summer time it is entirely dry. The Englishman was digging it deeper to take off the surface water when it came.

It is possible that, sometime, Indians had burned their captives there. In fact there is no doubt of it. It must have been the work of Indians. We may go back in our imaginations to the time, when the place where the city of Detroit now stands was an Indian town or village, and ask its inhabitants if they knew who were burned twelve miles west of there on a creek, they might not be able to tell. We might ask the giant Indian of the sand hill, if he knew, and he might say, "I had a hand in that; it was in my day." But we have no medium, through which we can find out the dark mysteries of the past. They will have to remain until the light of eternity dawns, and all the dead who have ever lived are called to be again, and to come forth. Then the dark mysteries of the past which have been locked up for centuries will be revealed.

CHAPTER XII.

THE INSIDE OF OUR HOUSE—
A PICTURE FROM MEMORY.

As I have been led away, for some years, following poor Indian in his belief, life and death, and in doing so have wandered from my story, I will now return to the second or third year of our settlement. I described how the body of our second house was made, and the roof put on. I now look at its interior. The lower floor was made of whitewood boards, in their rough state, nailed down. The upper floor was laid with the same kind of boards, though they were not nailed When they shrunk they could be driven together, to close the cracks. The chimney was what we called a "stick" or "Dutch chimney." The way it was built; two crooked sticks, six inches wide and four inches thick, were taken for arms; the foot of these sticks were placed on the inner edge or top of the second log of the house, and the upper ends laid against the front beam of the chamber floor. These sticks or arms were about six feet apart at the mouth of the chimney. Father cut a green black oak and sawed off some bolts, took a froe, that he brought from York State, and rived out shakes three inches wide and about an inch thick. Of these and clay he laid up the chimney. It started from the arms and the chamber beam. After it got up a little it was like laying up a pen. He spread on some clay, then laid on four sticks and pressed them into the clay, then spread on clay again, covering the sticks entirely. In this way our chimney was built, and its size, at the top, was about two by four feet. It proved to be quite a good and safe chimney.

The last thing before retiring for the night, after the fire had burned low and the big coals were covered with ashes, was to look up chimney and see if it had taken fire. If it had, and was smoking on the inside, father would take a ladder, set it up in the chimney, take a little water and go up and put it out. This was seldom necessary, as it never took fire unless the clay cracked in places, or the weather wore it off.

When there was a small fire in the evening, I could stand on the clay hearth and look through the chimney at the stars as they twinkled and shone in their brightness. I could count a number of them as I stood there. Father drove into a log, back of the fire place, two iron eyes on which to hang a crane; they extended into the room about one foot. Around, and at one side of these he built the back of the fireplace of clear clay a foot thick at the bottom, but thinner when it got up to the sticks; after the clay dried he hung the crane. It is seen that we had no jambs to our fireplace. Father sometimes at night would get a backlog in. I have seen those which he got green, and very large, which were sometimes twenty inches through and five or six feet long. When he got the log to the door, he would take a round stick as large as his arm, lay it on the floor, so that his log would come crossways of it, and then crowd the log. I have seen him crowd it with a handspike and the stick would roll in opposite the fireplace. He would tell us children to stand back and take the chairs out of the way. Then he would roll the log into the fireplace, and very carefully so as not to break or crack the clay hearth, for mother had all the care of that, and wished it kept as nicely as possible. When he had the log on to suit him, he would say, "There, I guess that will last awhile." Then he would bring in two green sticks, six or eight inches through and about three feet long, and place them on the hearth with the ends against the backlog. These he called his Michigan andirons; said he was proud of them. He said they were wood instead of iron, to be sure, but he could afford to have a new pair whenever he wanted them. When he brought in a large fore-stick, and laid it across his andirons, he had the foundation for a fire, for twenty-four hours.

On the crane hung two or three hooks, and on these, over the fire, mother did most of her cooking. As we had no oven, mother had what we called a bake kettle; this was a flat, low kettle, with a cast cover, the rim of which turned up an inch or two, to hold coals. In this kettle, she baked our bread. The way she did it; she would heat the lid, put her loaf of bread in the kettle, take the shovel and pull out some coals on the hearth, set the kettle on them, put the lid on and shovel some coals on to it. Then she would watch it, turn it round a few times, and the bread was done, and it came on the table steaming. When we all gathered around the family board we did the bread good justice. We were favored with what we called "Michigan appetites." Sometimes when we had finished our meal there were but few fragments left, of anything except the loaf, which was four or five inches through, a foot and a half across, and four and a half feet in circumference.

Later, mother bought her a tin baker, which she placed before the fire to bake her bread, cake, pies, etc. This helped her very much in getting along. It was something new, and we thought it quite an invention. Mother had but one room, and father thought he would build an addition at the west end of our house, as the chimney was on the east end. He built it with a shed roof. The lower floor was made of boards, the upper floor of shakes. These were gotten out long enough to reach from beam to beam and they were lapped and nailed fast.

This room had one window on the west, and a door on the east, which led into the front room. In one corner stood a bed surrounded by curtains as white as snow; this mother called her spare-day bed. Two chests and a few chairs completed the furniture of this room; it was mother's sitting room and parlor. I remember well how pleased she was when she got a rag-carpet to cover the floor.

Now I have in my mind's eye a view of my mother's front room. Ah! there is the door on the south with its wooden latch and leather string.

East of the door is a window, and under it stands a wooden bench, with a water pail on it; at the side of the window hangs the tin dipper. In the corner beyond this stands the ladder, the top resting on one side of an opening through which we entered the chamber. In the centre of the east end burned the cheerful fire, at the left stood a kettle, pot and bread-kettle, a frying pan (with its handle four feet long) and griddle hung over them. Under the north window stood a table with its scantling legs, crossed, and its whitewood board top, as white as hands and ashes could scour it. Farther on, in the north-west corner stood mother's bed, with a white sheet stretched on a frame made for that purpose, over it, and another at the back and head. On the foot and front of the frame were pinned calico curtains with roses and rosebuds and little birds, some perched on a green vine that ran through the print, others on the wing, flying to and from their straw colored nests. These curtains hung, oh, how gracefully, around that bed! They were pinned back a little at the front, revealing a blue and white coverlet, of rare workmanship. In the next and last corner stood the family cupboard. The top shelves were filled with dishes, which mother brought from the state of New York. They were mostly blue and white, red and white and there were some on the top shelf which the children called their "golden edged dishes."

The bottom of the cupboard was inclosed; by opening two small doors I could look in. I found not there the luxuries of every clime, but what was found there was eaten with as much relish as the most costly viands would be now. It was a place I visited often. In hooks attached to a beam overhead hung two guns which were very frequently used. A splint broom and five or six splint bottomed chairs constituted nearly all the furniture of this room. Before that cheerful fire in one of those chairs, often sat one making and mending garments, little and big. This she did with her own hands, never having heard of a sewing machine, as there were none in existence then. She had to make every stitch with her fingers. We were not so fortunate as the favored people of ancient times; our garments would wax old.

Mother made a garment for father to work in which he called his frock. It was made of linen cloth that she brought from the State of New York. It was like a shirt only the sleeves were short. They reached half way to his elbows. This he wore, in place of a shirt, when working hard in warm weather. Southeast of the house father dug into the ground and made him an out door cellar, in which we kept our potatoes through the winter without freezing them. We found it very convenient.

Father wanted a frame barn very much but that was out of his reach. We needed some place to thrash, and to put our grain and hay, and where we could work in wet weather, but to have it was out of the question, so we did the next best thing, went at it and built a substitute. In the first place we cut six large crotches, went about fourteen rods north of the house, across the lane, dug six holes and set the two longest crotches in the center east and west. Then put the four shorter ones, two on the south and two on the north side so as to give the roof a slant. In the crotches we laid three large poles and on these laid small poles and rails, then covered the whole with buckwheat straw for a roof. We cut down straight grained timber, split the logs open and hewed the face and edges of them; we laid them back down on the ground, tight together and made a floor under the straw roof.

This building appeared from a distance something like a hay barrack. Now we had a sort of thrashing-floor. Back of this we built a log stable. So the north side was enclosed but the east and west ends and the south side were open. We had to have good weather when we threshed with our flails, as the snow or rain would blow right through it. It was a poor thing but the best we had for several years, until father was able, then he built him a good frame barn. It stands there on the old place yet (1875). I often think of the old threshing floor. When I got a nice buck with large horns I cut off the skull with the hide, so as to keep them in a natural position, and nailed them on the corners of our threshing floor in front. The cold and storms of winter did not affect them much. There they remained, mute and silent, to guard the place, and let all passers by know that a sort of a hunter lived there. Father had good courage and worked hard. He bared his arms and brow to the adverse winds, storms, disappointments, cares and labors of a life in the woods. He said, if he had his health, some day we would be better off. In a few years his words of encouragement proved true. He fought his way through manfully, like a veteran pioneer, raised up from poverty to peace and plenty. This he accomplished by hard labor, working days and sometimes nights.

One time father wanted to clear off a piece of ground for buckwheat by the first of July. He had not much time in which to do it. We had learned that buckwheat would catch and grow very stout on new and stumpy ground. Sometimes it filled very full and loaded heavy. It was easily gathered and easily threshed, and helped us very much for our winter's bread. One night after supper, father sat down and smoked his pipe; it was quite dark when he got up, took his ax in his hand and went out. We all knew where he had gone. It was to put up his log heaps, as he had some burning. Mother said, "We will go and help pick up and burn." When we started, looking towards the woods, we could see him dimly through the darkness. As we neared him we could see his bare arms with the handspike in his hands rolling up the logs. The fire took a new hold of them when he rolled them together. The flames would shoot up bright, and his countenance appeared to be a pale red, while thousands of sparks flew above his head and disappeared in the air. In a minute there was an awkward boy at his side with a handspike, taking hold and doing the best he could to help, and there was mother by the light of the fires, who a short time before in her native home, was an invalid and her life despaired of, now, with some of her children, picking up chips and sticks and burning them out of the way.

We were well rewarded for our labor. The buckwheat came up and in a little time it was all in bloom. It put on its snow white blossoms, and the wind that caressed it, and caused it to wave, bore away on its wings to the woods the fragrance of the buckwheat field.

The little industrious bee came there with its comrades and extracted its load of sweet, then flew back to its native home in the forest. There it deposited its load, stored it away carefully against the time of need. Nature taught the bee that a long, cold winter was coming and that it was best to work and improve the time, and the little fellow has left us a very bright example to follow.

CHAPTER XIII.

METHEGLIN OR THE DETECTED DRINK.

As will be remembered by the early settlers of Michigan, bee hunting and wild honey constituted one of the comforts and luxuries of life. Father being somewhat expert in finding bees found a number of trees, one of which was a large whitewood and stood full a mile or more, from home. One day he and I cut it down. It proved to be a very good tree, as far as honey was concerned. We easily filled our buckets and returned home, leaving a large quantity in the tree, which we intended to return and get as soon as possible. When we returned we found to our surprise, that the tree had caught fire and was burning quite lively where the honey was secreted. The fire originated from the burning of some straw that father had used in singeing the bees to prevent their ferocious attacks and stinging. We found that the fire had melted some of the honey and that it was running into a cavity in the tree which the bees had cleaned out. It looked as nice as though it had dripped into a wooden bowl. Father said there was a chance to save it, and we dipped out a pailful of nice clear honey, except that it was tinged, somewhat, in color and made a little bitter by the fire.

This formed one of the ingredients used in making the metheglin. We also secured some more very nice honey. Father said, judging from the amount we got, he should think the tree contained at least a hundred pounds of good honey, and I should think so too. And he said "This truly is a goodly land; it flows with milk and honey." He also said, "I will make a barrel of metheglin, which will be a very delicious drink for my family and a kind of a substitute for the luxuries they left behind. It will slake the thirst of the friendly pioneers, who may favor us with a call in our new forest home; or those friends who come to talk over the adventures of days now past, and the prospects of better days to come."

But in order to make the metheglin, he must procure a barrel, and this he had to bring some distance on his back, as we had no team. When he got the barrel home, and ready to make his metheglin, he located it across two sticks about three feet long and six inches through. These he placed with the ends toward the chimney on the chamber floor, and on them next to the chimney, he placed his barrel. He filled it with metheglin and said that the heat of the fire below, and warmth of the chimney above, would keep it from freezing. Being placed upon the sticks he could draw from it at his convenience, which he was quite sure to do when any of the neighbors called. Neighbors were not very plenty in those days and we were always glad to see them. When they came father would take his mug, go up the ladder and return with it filled with metheglin. Then he would pour out a glass, hand it to the neighbor, who would usually say, "What is it?" Father would say, "Try it and see." This they usually did. He then told them: "This is my wine, it was taken from the woods and it is a Michigan drink, the bees helped me to make it." It was generally called nice. Of course he frequently, after a hard day's work, would go up in the chamber, draw some and give us all a drink. It tasted very good to all, and especially to me, as will be seen by what follows. It so happened that the chamber where the barrel was kept, was the sleeping apartment of myself and brother, John S. I played the more important part in the "Detected drink;" at least I thought so.

I found, by examining the barrel, that by removing a little block, which was placed under the side, taking out the bung and putting my mouth in its place I could roll the barrel a little, on the sticks, and by being very careful, could get a drink with ease. Then replacing the bung and rolling the barrel back to its place, very carefully so as not to make a noise or arouse suspicion, I would put the block in its place thinking no one was any wiser, but me, for the drink which I thought was very palatable and delicious. Not like the three drinks I had taken from the jug some time before.

This continued for sometime very much to my comfort, as far as good drink was concerned. It was usually indulged in at night, after I had undressed my feet, and father and mother supposed I had retired. There was one difficulty. I was liable to be exposed by my little brother, John S., who slept with me; so I concluded to take him into my confidence. There were two reasons for my doing so: first, I wished him to have something good; and second, I wanted to have him implicated with myself, fearing that he might reveal my proceedings. So we enjoyed it together for a few nights. I would drink first, then hold the barrel for him while he drank. We thought we were faring like nabobs. But alas for me! One evening brother John S. and I retired as usual, leaving father and mother seated by the fire, I suppose talking over the scenes of their early days or, more probably, discussing the best way to get along and support their family in this their new forest home.

I thought, of course, we must have some of the good drink before we shut our eyes for the night, and no sooner thought than we went for it. As usual, I removed the block and out with the bung, then down with my mouth to the bung hole and over with the barrel until the delightful liquid reached my anxious lips. My thirst was soon slaked by a good drink, I relished it first rate.

Then came brother John S.' turn, and, some way, in attempting to get his drink I let the barrel slip. He was small and I had to hold it for him, but this time the barrel went. I grabbed for it, made some racket and some of the metheglin came out, guggle, guggle, good, good, and down it went to the chamber floor, which was made of loose boards. It ran through the cracks and there was a shower below, where father and mother were sitting. I was in a quandary. I knew I was doomed unless I could use some stratagem to clear myself from the scrape in which I was so nicely caught. When lo! the first thing I heard from below was father, apparently very angry, shouting, "William! what in the world are you doing with the metheglin barrel?" Then came my stratagem. I began to retch and make a noise as if vomiting, and hallooed to him that I was sick. Of course, I wanted to make him believe that it was the contents of my stomach that was falling at his feet in place of the metheglin. He said he knew better, it was too sudden an attack, and too much of a shower of the metheglin falling at their feet. I found that I could not make this ruse work. He started for me, his head appeared above the top of the ladder, he had a candle and a gad in his hand. I had been glad to see him often, before, and was afterward, but this time I saw nothing in him to admire. I found I had entirely failed. I told him that I would not do that again. "Oh honestly!" if he would only let me off, I would never do that again.

He would not hear one word I said, but seized hold of my arm and laid it on. Then there might have been heard a noise outside, and for some distance, like some striking against a boy about my size, if there had been any one around to have heard it. He said he did not whip me so much for the metheglin, as for lying and trying to deceive him. I do not think I danced a horn but I did step around lively, maybe, a little on tip He said, he thought he had cured me up, that the application he gave would make me well. I crawled into bed very much pleased indeed to think the mat was settled, as far as I was concerned. John S. had crawled into bed while I was paying the penalty. Father excused him because he was so young; he said I was the one to blame, and must stand it all. I thought as all young Americans do that it was rather hard to get such a tanning in Michigan, and I had begun to think myself quite a somebody.

From that day, or night, I made up my mind that honesty was the best policy, at all events, for me. When I went to bed, at night, after that I gave the metheglin barrel a wide berth and a good letting alone, for I had lost my relish for metheglin. The metheglin story is once in a while, until this day, related by John S., especially when we all meet for a family visit. It not unfrequently causes much laughter. I suppose the laughter is caused as much by the manner in which he tells it (he trying to imitate or mimic me) as its funniness. It sometimes causes a tear, perhaps, from excessive laughter and may be, from recollections of the past and its associations. It may once in a while cause me to give a dry laugh, but never a sad tear since the night I spilt the metheglin.

One way the bee-hunter took of finding bee trees was to go into the woods, cut a sappling off, about four feet from the ground, square the top of the stump and on this put a dish of honey in the comb. Then he would take his ax, cut and clear away the brush around the place so that he could see the bees fly and be able to get their course or line them. This he called a bee stand. In the fall of the year, when there came a warm, clear and sunny day, after the frost had killed the leaves and flowers, and the trees were bare, was the best time to find bee trees. Sometimes when father and I went bee-hunting he took some old honey comb, put it on a piece of bark or on a log, set it on fire and dropped a few drops of anise on it from a vial. If we were near a bee tree in a short time a lone bee would come. When it came it would fly around a few times and then light on the honey comb in the dish which it had scented. No doubt, it had been out industriously hunting and now it had found just what was desired. Very independently it would commence helping itself and get as much as it could possibly carry off to its home. Then it went and, no doubt, astonished some of its comrades with its large load of wealth. It was obtained so quickly and easily and there was plenty more where it came from. Then some of the other bees would accompany it back, all being very anxious to help in securing the honey they had found ready made. In a short time there were several bees in the dish and others were coming and going; then it was necessary for us to watch them. It required sharp strong eyes to get their line. They would rise and circle around, higher and higher, until they made out their course and then start like a streak straight for their colony. After we had staked or marked out the line the next thing was to move the honey forty or fifty rods ahead. At this the bees sometimes appeared a little suspicious. It was sometimes necessary to make a few of them prisoners even while they were eating by slipping a cover over them, and moving them ahead on the line. This made them a little shy, however, but they soon forgot their imprisonment. They had found too rich a store to be forsaken. After a little while they would come flocking back and load themselves as heavily as before. If they flew on in the same direction it was evident that the bee tree was still ahead, and it was necessary to move the honey again. Then if the bees flew crooked and high and zigzag it was plain to the bee-hunters that they were in close proximity to the bee tree. When the hunters could get sight of the bees going back or up towards the tree tops it was an easy matter to find the bee tree, as that would be between the two stands or right in the hunter's presence.

The little bees had, by their unceasing industry and through their love of gain, labored hard extracting their sweet and had laid it up carefully. Now they pointed out their storehouse by going directly to it when anxious eyes were watching them. The little aeronautic navigators could be seen departing from and returning to their home. Sometimes they went into a small hole in the side of the tree and at other times they entered their homes by a small knot-hole in a limb near the top of the tree. I saw that a swarm which father once found went into the tree top more than eighty feet from the ground. At that distance they did not appear larger than house-flies.

The first thing that father did after finding a bee-tree was to mark it by cutting the initials of his name on the bark with his pocket-knife. This established his title to the bees. After that they had a legal owner. The mark on the tree was one of the witnesses. I knew a man who happened to find a bee tree, and said that he marked it close down to the ground and covered the mark with leaves so that no one could find it. That appeared more sly than wise, as it gave no notice to others, who might find the tree, of his ownership, or of its having been previously found.

CHAPTER XIV.

OUR ROAD AND HOW I WAS WOUNDED.

Father got our road laid out and districted for a mile and a half on the north and south section line. One mile north of our place it struck the Dearborn road. Father cut it out, cut all the timber on the road two rods wide. After it was cut out I could get on the top of a stump in the road, by the side of our place, and look north carefully among the stumps, for a minute, and if there was any one coming, on the road, I could distinguish them from the stumps by seeing them move. In fact we thought we were almost getting out into the world. We could see the sand hill where father finally bought and built his house. Father was pathmaster for a number of years and he crosswayed the lowest spots and across the black ash swales. He cut logs twelve feet long and laid them side by side across the center of the road. Some of the logs, that he put into the road on the lowest ground, were more than a foot through; of course smaller poles answered where the ground was higher. We called this our corduroy road. In doing our road work and others doing theirs, year after year, in course of time we had the log way built across the wettest parts of the road. When it was still I could hear a cart or wagon, coming or going, rattling and pounding over the logs for nearly a mile. But it was so much better than water and mud that we thought it quite passable. We threw some clay and dirt on to the logs and it made quite an improvement, especially in a dry time. But in a wet time it was then, and is now, a very disagreeable road to travel, as the clay gathers on the feet of the pedestrian, until it is a load for him to carry. This gave it, in after times, the name of the "Hardscrabble Road." When it was wet it was almost impossible to get through with a team and load. At such times we had to cross Mr. Pardee's place and go around the ridge on a road running near the old trail. Now the "Hardscrabble Road" is an old road leading to the homes of hundreds. Sometimes there may be seen twelve or fifteen teams at once on the last half mile of that road, besides footmen, coming and going all in busy life. They little know the trouble we once had there in making that road.

Father had very hard work to get along. He had to pay Mrs. Phlihaven twenty-seven dollars every year to satisfy her on the mortgage, as he was not able to pay the principal. That took from us what we needed very much. If we could have had it to get us clothes it would have helped us, as we were all poorly clad. Some of the younger children went barefooted all winter a number of times. I often saw their little barefooted tracks in the snow.

As we had no team we had to get along the best we could. Father changed work with Mr. Pardee: he came with his oxen and plowed for us. Father had to work two days for one, to pay him. In this way we got some plowing done. There was a man by the name of Stockman who lived near Dearbornville. He had a pair of young oxen. Being a carpenter, by trade, he worked at Detroit some of the time. He would let father use his oxen some of the time for their keeping, and that he might break them better, as they were not thoroughly broken. They would have been some profit to us it they had not crippled me.

One day I was drawing logs with them. I had hitched the chain around a log and they started. I hallooed, "Whoa!" but they wouldn't stop. They swung the log against me, caught my leg between the log they were drawing and the sharp end of another log and had me fast. It cut the calf of my leg nearly in two, and tore the flesh from the bone, but did not break it. I screamed and made an awful ado. Father and Mr. Purdy heard me and came running as fast as they could, they took me up and carried me to the house. It was over three long months before I could take another step with that leg. This accident made it still harder for father. I know I saved him a good many steps and some work. I am sure he was pleased when I got over my lameness and so I could help him again. I took a great interest in everything he did and helped him all I could.

Finally father got a chance to work by the day, for the government, at Dearbornville. He received six shillings a day in silver. He said he would leave me, to do what I could on the place, and he would try working for Uncle Sam a part of the time. In haying and harvesting he had to work at home. He cut all the grass himself and it grew very stout. We found our land was natural for timothy and white clover. The latter would come up thick in the bottom, of itself, and make the grass very heavy. It was my business to spread the hay and rake it up. In this way we soon got through with our haying and harvesting. We had already seeded some land down for pasture. We went to Dearbornville and got hayseed off of a barn floor and scattered it on the ground, in this way we seeded our first pasture. Father sometimes let a small piece of timothy stand until it got ripe. Then took his cradle, cut it and I tied it up in small bundles and then stood it up until it was dry. When dry it was thrashed out; in this way we soon had plenty of grass seed of our own, without having to buy it. We began to have quite a stock of cows and young cattle. We had pasture for them a part of the time, but sometimes we had to let them run in the woods. At night I would go after them. When I got in sight of them I would count them, to see if they were all there. The old cow (which had been no small part of our support and our stand-by through thick and thin) would start and the rest followed her. When they were strung along ahead of me and I was driving them I would think to myself: now we've got quite a herd of cattle! From our first settlement mother wanted to, and did, raise every calf.

Father worked for the government what time he could spare. He had to go two miles morning and night. He carried his dinner in a little tin pail with a cover on it. When the days were short he had to start very early, and when he returned it would be in the evening, I recollect very well some things that he worked at. The arsenal and other buildings were up when we came here. They built a large brick wall from building to building, making the yard square. The top of the wall was about level. I think this wall was built twelve or fifteen feet high, it incloses three or four acres. There thousands of soldiers put on their uniforms and with their bright muskets in their hands and knapsacks strapped upon their backs drilled and marched to and fro. There they prepared themselves for the service of the country and to die, if need be, in defending the old flag of stars and stripes which waved there above their heads. Little thought they that the ground under their feet, so beautiful and level inside that yard was made ground, in some places for six or eight feet deep, and that it was done at Uncle Sam's expense for the pleasure of his boys in blue. It was their school yard in which to learn the science of war. My father helped to grade this enclosure. They drew in sand from the sand ridge back of the yard, from where the government barn now stands, with one-horse carts.

Father was very fond of Indian bread which he called "Johnny cake." When mother had wheat bread for the rest of us she often baked a "Johnny cake" for him. One day he took a little "Johnny cake," a cup of butter and some venison, in his little tin pail, for his dinner. He left it as usual in the workshop. At noon he partook of his humble repast. He said he left a piece of his "Johnny cake" and some butter. He thought that would make him a lunch at night, when his day's work was done and he started home. He went for his pail and found that his lunch was gone, and in place of it a beautiful pocket knife.

He said there were two or three government officers viewing and inspecting the arsenal and ground that day. He said they went into the shop where he left his dinner pail and lunch. He was sure they were the ones who took his lunch. He said they knew what was good, for they ate all the "Johnny cake" and butter he had left. The knife was left open and he thought they forgot and left it through mistake. But I think more probably they knew something of father's history.

He was one who would have been noticed in a crowd of workmen. I have no doubt the boss told them that he was a splendid workman. That he had had bad luck, that he lived on a new place, two or three miles back in the woods, that he had a large family to support and came clear out there every day to work. "Here is his dinner pail" one says, "let's look in it" and what did they see but a piece of Indian bread and some butter? Methinks, one of the officers might have said: "I have not eaten any of that kind of bread since my mother baked it down in New England. Let's try it." Then took out his knife, cut it in three or four pieces, spread the butter on and they ate it. Then he said, "Here is my knife, worth twelve shillings, I will leave it open; he shall have it. I will give it him as an honorary present, for his being a working man, and to compensate him for what we have eaten. It has reminded me of home." Now if the view I have taken is correct, it shows that they were noble, generous and manly; that they felt for the poor, in place of trifling with their feelings.

After father finished working there, he sold some young cattle and managed in some way to buy another yoke of oxen. We had good hay for them. Father went to the village and bought him a new wagon. It was a very good iron axletree wagon, made in Dearbornville by William Halpin. We were very much pleased to have a team again and delighted with our new wagon.

We had very good luck with these oxen and kept them until we got a horse team, and in fact longer, for after I left my father's house (and I was twenty-two years old when I left) he had them. Then he said his place was cleared up, and the roots rotted enough so that he could get along and do his work with horses. He sold his oxen to Mr. Purdy, and they were a good team then.

CHAPTER XV.

PROSPECT OF WAR—A.D. 1835.

The dark portentous cloud seemed to hang above our horizon. It looked dark and threatening, (and more terrible because the disputants were members of the same family). We thought it might break upon our heads at any time. The seat of war being so near us, the country so new and inhabitants so few, made it look still more alarming to me. I asked father how many inhabitants we had in our territory and how many the State of Ohio contained. He said there were as many as fifteen or twenty to our one. I asked him if he thought the Michigan men would be able to defend Toledo against so many. He said that Michigan was settled by the bravest men. That almost every man owned a rifle and was a good shot for a pigeon's head. He thought they would be able to keep them at bay until the government would interfere and help us. He said, to, that Governor Mason was a fearless, brave, courageous man. That he had called for militia and volunteers and was going himself with General Brown, at the head of his men, to defend the rights of Michigan.

One day, about this time, I was at Dearbornville; they had a fife and drum there and were beating up for militia and volunteers. A young man by the name of William Ozee had volunteered. I was well acquainted with him; he had been at our house frequently. Sometimes, in winter, he had chopped for us and I had hunted with him. He had a good rifle and was certainly a sharp shooter. I found that he beat me handily, but I made up my mind it was because he had a better rifle and I was considerable younger than he. I saw him at Dearbornville just before he went away. He told me to tell my folks that he was a soldier and was going to the war to defend them; that Governor Mason had called for troops and he was going with him. We heard in a short time that he was at Toledo. We also learned that Governor Lucas, of Ohio, with General Bell and staff, with an army of volunteers, all equipped ready for war, had advanced as far as Fort Miami. But Governor Mason was too quick for the Ohio Governor. He called upon General Brown to raise the Michigan militia, and said that his bones might bleach at Toledo before he would give up one foot of the territory of Michigan; said he would accompany the soldiers himself, to the disputed ground. He, with General Brown, soon raised a force of about a thousand men and took possession of Toledo; while the Governor of Ohio, with volunteers, was fooling away the time at Fort Miami. When we heard that Governor Mason had arrived at Toledo, we wondered if we should hear the roar of his cannon. Sometimes I listened. We thought if it was still and the wind favorable, we might hear them, and we expected every day there would be a battle.

But when Governor Lucas learned how determined Governor Mason was, and that he had at his back a thousand Michigan braves, and most of them with their rifles in their hands, ready to receive him, he made up his mind that he had better let them alone. We afterward learned that Governor Lucas only had six or eight hundred men. The conclusion was, that if they had attacked the Michigan boys at Toledo, they would have gotten badly whipped, and those of them left alive would have made good time running for the woods, and would have wished that they had never heard of Michigan men. Perhaps the Ohio Governor thought that discretion was the better part of valor. He employed his time for several days, watching over the line. May be he employed some of his time thinking if it could be possible that Governor Mason and General Brown were going to subjugate Ohio, or at least a part of it, and annex it to the territory of Michigan.

Let this be as it may; while he seemed to be undecided, two commissioners from Washington put in an appearance and remonstrated with him. They told him what the fearful consequences, to him and his State, would be, if he tried to follow out his plan to gain possession of the disputed territory. These commissioners held several conferences with both Governors. They submitted to them several propositions for their consideration, and for the settlement of the important dispute. Their proposition was this: that the inhabitants, residing on the disputed ground, should be left to their own government. Obeying one or the other, as they might prefer, without being disturbed by the authorities of either Michigan or Ohio. They were to remain thus until the close of the next session of Congress. Here we see the impossibility of man being subjected to and serving two masters, for, "He will love the one and hate the other, or hold to the one and despise the other."

Governor Lucas was glad to get out of the scrape. He embraced the proposition, disbanded his men and left the disputed ground. Governor Mason considered himself master of the situation; Toledo and the disputed territory were under his control. He would not compromise the rights of his people, and he considered that it rightly belonged to Michigan. He disbanded a part of his force and sent them home, but kept enough organized so that he could act in case of emergency. He kept an eagle eye upon the "Buckeyes" to see that our territorial laws were executed promptly and they were executed vigorously. In doing it one Michigan man was wounded, his would-be murderer ran away to Ohio and was protected by Governor Lucas. The man who was wounded was a deputy-sheriff of Monroe County. He was stabbed with a knife. His was the only blood spilled. Some few surveyors and Ohio sympathizers were arrested and put into jail at Monroe. But Uncle Sam put his foot down, to make peace in the family. He said if we would submit, after awhile we might shine as a star in the constellation of the Union. So we were promised a star in a prominent place in the old flag and territory enough, north of us, for a State. To be sure it is not quite so sunny a land as that near Toledo, and our Governor and others did not like to acquiesce in the decision of the government, yet they had to yield to Uncle Sam's superior authority.

Then they did not imagine that the upper peninsula was so rich a mining country. They little knew at that time that its very earth contained, in its bosom and under its pure waters, precious metals, iron, copper and silver enough to make a State rich. Finally our people consented and the Territory of Michigan put on her glory as a State. Became a proud member of the Union; her star was placed in the banner of the free. It has since sparkled upon every sea and been seen in every port throughout the civilized world, as the emblem of the State of Michigan.

In the excitement of the Toledo war we looked upon the Ohio men unfavorably. We were interested for ourselves, and might have been somewhat selfish and conceited, and, maybe, jealous of our neighbors, and thought them wrong in the fray. We had forgotten that there were then men living in Ohio, in log houses and cabins, some of them as brave men as ever walked the footstool; that they came to Michigan and rescued the country from the invaders, the English and savages, long before some of us knew that there was such a place as Michigan. When Michigan was almost a trackless wilderness they crossed Lake Erie, landed at Malden, drove the redcoats out of the fort and started them on the double quick. They made for the Canadian woods, and the British and Indians, who held Detroit, followed suit. They were followed by our brave William Henry Harrison, accompanied by Ohio and Kentucky men to the Thames. There, at one blow, the Americans subjected the most of Upper Canada and punished the invaders of Michigan, who had the hardihood to set their hostile feet upon her territory. It seems as though it must have been right that the strip of country at Toledo was given to the brave men, some at least of whom long years before, defended it with their lives and helped to raise again the American flag at Detroit.

In about five years from the time of the Toledo War, William Henry Harrison, of Ohio, was nominated, by the Whig party, for President, and John Tyler, of Virginia, for Vice President, of the United States. The intelligence spread like wild-fire. It went from town to town and from county to county, through the brand-new State of Michigan. General Harrison appeared to be the coming man. The Whigs of Ohio and Michigan met and shook hands, like brothers, over the difficulties of the past; now they had a more patriotic undertaking before them. In union with the rest of the Whig party of the United States, they were to elect the old farmer of the West, the good man who loved his country. In its defence he had won imperishable honors. After he laid down his armor he resided in a log house and was often clad in the habiliments of a husbandman. Now he was nominated for President of the United States. With such a candidate for the presidency men's hearts leaped for joy in anticipation of a victory at the ballot-box in the fall of 1840.

The nomination of General Harrison raised quite an excitement throughout the entire country. Even in Dearborn, what few Whigs there were in the town united as one man, entered upon the campaign and banded themselves together to work for the good of the Whig party. Alonzo T. Mather was one who stood at the head of the party in Dearborn. He was a man noted for his good religious principles, and was one of the most prominent and influential citizens of the town. He was sent to the Legislature, at Detroit, for Wayne county, one term and held other offices of trust and honor. He was the chieftain of his party and one of the prime movers in getting up a log cabin in Dearborn. This log cabin was built on large truck wheels. When finished it appeared somewhat the shape of a log car. It was thought necessary to have something on board to eat and drink. It was desired to make all typical and commemorative of the veteran, pioneer, farmer and general who had escaped the bullets of the savages at Tippecanoe, although he was a special mark for them, without a scar and the loss only of a lock of hair, which was clipped off by a bullet. This, too, was the man who shared his own supplies with his soldiers when they were reduced to the necessity of eating horse flesh. Now, in honor to such a man, the Whig bakers of Dearborn made a "Johnny cake" at least ten feet long and the width of it was in proportion to the length. They patted it with care, smoothed it over nicely and baked it before the fire. It was a good, plump cake, and nothing like it was ever seen in Dearborn, before or since. Careful hands put it on board the log cabin, also a barrel of hard cider was put on board.

At this time, although the country was new, politics ran high in Dearborn. A friendly invitation was sent around to the farmers to come, at a certain time, with their ox-teams and help draw the log cabin to its destination and accompany the Whig delegation with it to Detroit. I knew one Democrat who, when invited, refused to go. He appeared to be rather eccentric. He said, "I allow that my oxen are not broke to work on either side, and they are too Democratic to pull on both sides of the fence at one and the same time." He considered the excitement of the people, their building log cabins and baking such "Johnny cakes" boyish and foolish. He said, in fact, that those who were doing it were "on the wrong side." Many of the Democratic frontier men admired General Harrison for his great worth as a man and liked his having a national reputation for bravery. They said he was an honor to America as an American citizen and soldier, but that he was on the wrong side.

At that time I was in my teens and looking anxiously forward for time to help me to the elective franchise. Perhaps, I should state here that father was a Democrat as long ago as I can remember. In York State he was a strong Jackson man and coming into the woods of Michigan did not change his political principles. He was an irrepressible Democrat and remained one. Jackson was his ideal statesman. When he went to Dearbornville to attend town meeting or election, he almost invariably carried a hickory cane, with the bark on it as it grew, in honor of "Old Hickory." He was always known by his townsmen as a staunch Democrat. It was natural for his young family, to claim to be Democrats in principle, in their isolated home.

The first settlers in our neighborhood, on the Ecorse, were Democrats, with one exception, and that one was Mr. Blare. He often visited at our house, and to tease my little brother, then five or six years old, told him that he must be a Whig, he would make a good one, that he was a Whig, he appeared like one and so forth. Brother denied it stoutly and said that he would not be a Whig for any one. This amused Mr. Blare very much for some time. Finally, when he called one day, he said he was going to have company, he could see plainly that J.S. was changing to a Whig very fast. J.S. denied it as strongly as ever, but it was evident that the idea of being a Whig troubled him greatly. One morning (a short time after Mr. Blare had been talking to him) he was crying bitterly. Mother said she thought it very strange that he should cry so and tried sometimes, in vain, to persuade him to tell her what the trouble was. Finally she threatened to punish him if he did not let her know what the difficulty was. At last he said he was afraid he was turning to be a Whig. Mother assured him that it was not so. She said there was no danger of her little boy changing into a Whig, not in the least. J.S. has often been reminded, since he became a man, of the time Mr. Blare came so near making a Whig of him.

But back to that cabin. There were plenty of men who volunteered and took their teams. They hitched a long string of them, I think twenty-two yoke of oxen, to the trucks. Quite a large crowd, for Dearborn, of old and young, were on hand to witness the start. Most of them appeared very enthusiastic. Each gave vent to some expression of admiration like the following: "The General is the man for me;" or, "He is one of the people, one with the people, one for the people, one with us and we are for him." That's my sentiment, said one and another. After such exclamations and the singing of a spirited campaign song, the order was given to start the teams. The large wheels rolled and the log cabin began to move. Nearly all appeared to be excited and there was some confusion of voices. Cheer after cheer arose clear and high for the honest old farmer of North Bend. I learned afterward that the march to Detroit was one continued ovation.

As a matter of course, I didn't go with them. I was too busy, at that time, taking lessons and studying my politics, and all that sort of thing at home in the woods.

CHAPTER XVI.

FISHING AND BOATING.

In the spring of the year when the ice broke up, in the creek, the (pike) or (pickerel) came up in great abundance from Detroit River, and they were easily caught. At such times the water was high in the creek, often overflowing its banks. Sometimes the Ecorse appeared like quite a river. We made a canoe of a white-wood log and launched it on the Ecorse. Sometimes we went fishing in the canoe. At such times it needed two, as the pickerel were fond of lying in shallow water or where there was old grass. By looking very carefully, on the surface of the water, I could see small ripples that the fishes made with their fins while they were sporting in their native element. By having a person in the back end of the canoe, pole it carefully, toward the place where I saw the ripples, we would get up in plain sight of them, and they could be either speared or shot.

I think the most successful way was shooting them, at least I preferred it. If the fish lay near the surface of the water, I held the gun nearly on it, and if it was six inches deep I held the gun six inches under it, and fired. In this way, for the distance of two or three rods, I was sure to kill them or stun them so that they turned belly up and lay till they were easily picked up with a spear. In this way I frequently caught a nice string. I have caught some that would weigh eight pounds apiece. Sometimes I stood on a log that lay across the creek and watched for them when they were running up. I recollect one cloudy afternoon I fished with a spear and I caught as many as I wanted to carry to the house. Sometimes they would be in a group of three, four or more together. I have seen them, with a big fish below, and four or five smaller ones above him, swimming along together as nicely as though they had been strung on an invisible string, and drawn along quietly through the water. I could see their wake as they were coming slowly up the creek keeping along one side of it. When I first saw them in the water they looked dark, I saw it was a group of fishes. It looked as though the smaller ones were guarding the larger one, at least they were accompanying it. They appeared to be very good friends, and well acquainted, and none of them afraid of being eaten up, but any of them would have eagerly caught the smaller ones of another species and swallowed them alive and whole. I do not know that they devour and eat their own kind, I think not often, for nature has given the pickerel, when young and small, the ability to move with such swiftness that it would be impossible for a larger fish to catch them. They will be perfectly still in the water, and if scared by anything they will start away in any direction like a streak. They go as if it were no effort and move with the rapidity of a dart. I have cut some of the large pickerel open and found whole fish in them, five or six inches long.

But I must finish describing that group of fishes! As they were swimming up, the smaller ones kept right over the large one. I stood until they got almost to me and I killed four of them at once and got them all. It is known that it is not necessary to hit a fish with a bullet in order to get it. It is the force of the bullet, or charge, striking the water that shocks or stuns him, and causes him to turn up.

These fish ran up two or three weeks every spring. Then those which were not caught went back again into the Detroit River. Father made him what he called a pike net which had two wings. By the time the fish were running back, the water was settled into the bed of the creek. Then father would set his net in the creek, stretch the wings across and stake it fast. The mouth of the net opened up stream. This he called a funnel; it was shaped like the top of a funnel. It was fastened with four hoops. The first one was about as large around as the hoop of a flour barrel, the next smaller, the third smaller still, and the last one was large enough for the largest fish to go through.

When the net was fastened around these hoops it formed a tunnel about four feet long. Then we had a bag net eight or ten feet long. The mouth of this was tied around the first or large hoop of the tunnel, so when the fish came down and ran into that they could not find their way out. Father said when the fish were running back to Detroit River, it was right to catch them, but when they were going up everybody along the creek ought to have a chance. I never knew him to put his net in, so long as the fish were running up. When they got to going back, as they most all run in the night, in the evening he would go and set his net, and next morning he would have a beautiful lot of fish. In this way, some springs, we caught more than we could use fresh, so salted some down for summer use. They helped us very much, taking the place of other meat. For years back there have hardly any fish made their appearance up the Ecorse. Now it would be quite a curiosity to see one in the creek. I suppose the reason they do not come up is that some persons put in gill nets at the mouth of the Ecorse, on Detroit River, and catch them, or stop them at least. It is known that fish will not run out of a big water, and run up a small stream, at any time except in the night.

These denizens of the deep have their own peculiar ways, and although man can contrive to catch them, yet he cannot fathom the mysteries that belong alone to them. Where they travel he cannot tell for they leave no track behind.

It is seen that I used a hunter's phrase in my description of holding the gun while shooting fish. The hunter will readily understand it as given. If he has seen a deer and it has escaped him, and you ask him why he didn't shoot it; he almost invariably says, "I couldn't get my gun on it before it jumped out of my sight." To such as do not understand that phrase I will say, the expression is allowable, as the bullet or charge of shot flies so swiftly (even in advance of the sharp report of the gun). The distance of twenty rods or more is virtually annihilated: Hence the expression,

"I held the gun on it," (though it was rods away.) If he sighted his gun straight toward the object he wished to hit whether it was in the air, under water, or on the ground, he would claim that he held his gun on it.

I said that the bullet flew in advance of the report of the gun. That is true, on the start, or until it struck an object. If the object was at a reasonable distance, but if the distance proved too far, it of course would fall behind the sound. The bullet is the bold—fearless—and often cruel companion of the report of the gun, and loses in its velocity the farther it flies, being impeded and resisted by the air, and at last is left flattened and out of shape, a dead weight, while the report of the gun passes on very swiftly, and dies away in the distance to be heard no more. I have often heard the reports of guns very plainly that were fired at ducks on Detroit River, six or seven miles away. With what velocity their sounds approached me, I leave Dr. Derham to determine. According to his calculation it must have been at the rate of eleven hundred and forty-two feet per second. It has also been ascertained with what velocity the ball leaves the gun and pierces the air. The following is the practical result ascertained by the experiments of Mr. Robins, Count Rumford, and Dr. Hutton: "A musket ball, discharged with a common charge of powder, issues from the muzzle of the piece with a velocity between sixteen and seventeen hundred feet in a second."

CHAPTER XVII.

HOW I GOT IN TROUBLE RIDING IN A CANOE.

I often rode in my canoe when I did not go fishing. I took one ride in it that I shall always remember, at least the remembrance of it has forced itself upon my mind a number of times, in the days gone by, and I expect to think of it a few times more. Of course my oldest sister, Rachel, who is now Mrs. Crandell, of Dearborn, became acquainted with the young ladies of the neighborhood. One fine afternoon, in the spring of the year when the water was high, two of her friends came to see her. They were considered very fine young ladies. One was Miss Lucy Lord, the other I will call nameless, but she is an old resident and lives near by. If at any time this should meet her eye she will vouch for the truth of it. They came to spend the afternoon with sister.

Of course (as all young men do, I believe) I felt a little flattered, and thought, no doubt, one object of their visit was to see me. Whether my humble self was once in all their thoughts, when they were making their toilet that day or not, I gave them the credit of it. I thought I had never seen one of them, at least, look any better than she did that afternoon. Her hair was arranged very nicely and she was very graceful. Of course, when my sister told me they wished very much for a boat ride, I could not very well to refuse to go with them. I hoped to let them see with how much skill I could manage my canoe. But alas for my skill! The flat was covered with water from our little ridge to the creek, a distance of twenty rods. It looked like a large river. The canoe was anchored near the ridge; the young ladies got in and we started from the landing. I had to look out for the stumps and hummocks so as not to run against them nor run my boat aground. I had my passengers aboard and I stood in the hind end of the canoe, and with a hand pole I set it along with greater rapidity than it could have been paddled. We glided over the water, on the flat, amid the joyful acclamations and gleeful laughter of my fair companions. One said, "I haven't had a boat ride before in Michigan." Miss Lucy, who sat on the bow end of the boat, waved her handkerchief and said, "Oh, bless me! isn't this pleasant, sailing on the water!" Another said, "How nice we go!" Of course I propelled along with considerable speed. I thought I had one of the nicest, prettiest and most intelligent load of passengers that had ever been in my canoe or on that water, and I would give them a nice ride.

At last we got round as far as the creek. There the water ran more swiftly than it did on the flat. I told the young ladies I thought we had better not try to navigate that, but they all said, "Let us ride up the creek!" I thought I was master of the situation and could manage the canoe. I did not want to tell them that I was afraid, for fear they would say I was fainthearted. I thought that would be very much against me, and as I had such a brave crew, I made up my mind to go up the strong current. I turned the bow of the boat up against the current, as much as I could with one hold, but could not get it straight against the current. It shot ahead its length or more, then I moved my hand pole to get a new hold. Now we were over the creek and the water being four or five feet deep, it was impossible for me to get my pole down to the bottom again in time to save us. While I was trying to do that, the current being stronger than I supposed, turned the boat sidewise. I saw that we were gone for it. The girls sprang to one side of the boat and down we went, at one plunge, all together into the water. My craft was foundered, filled with water and went down, (stream at least). Miss Lucy Lord was the heroine of the occasion; luckily, she saved herself by jumping, though she got very wet. She got on to a little hummock on the bank and was on terra-firma.

As soon as I took in the situation, I exerted myself to save the rest of the crew. The nameless girl's head came in sight about the same time my own did. As soon as she could halloo she said, "Lord have mercy! Lord help!" Miss Lucy held out her hand and said, "Come here and Lord will help you." I helped her and my sister to the bank as quickly as possible. I had to be very lively in securing the white pocket handkerchief that had been our flag while sailing.

After they got fairly out, they started like three deer, as three dears they were, for the house, each one for herself. The way they made three wakes through that water was something new to me. I had never seen the like of that before. Miss Lucy went ahead full of life. They went through the water from one to two feet deep all the way to the ridge. There were father, mother and all the rest, to witness their safe arrival on the shore, and join them in their merry, though I think sad laugh. I knew it would all be laid to me. After I watched them to the house and knew they were very jolly, I started for the canoe. It had gone down in the water to a large log that lay across the creek and lodged against it.

I was as wet as I could be, and I jumped in again, drew it from the log and pulled it along full of water, up the creek, until I got where the bank was a little higher. Then I drew the front end up and the water ran over the back end. When it was so that I could tow it, I took it across the flat in front of the house, and left it there in its place. Then I went in the house. They had coined a brand new title for me; they called me "Captain." They said I had come near drowning my passengers. Mother said it was not safe for young ladies to ride with me on the water. Father said, he thought I was not much of a sailor, that I did not understand navigation; and I made up my mind that he was correct, that I was not much of a water-man.

CHAPTER XVIII.

OUR CLEARING AND THE FIRST RAILROAD CARS IN 1838.

Our prospects began to brighten a little, and it is needless for me to attempt to describe what our feelings were, when we got a strip of the primeval forest cleared away. Our clearing now extended across the two lots, being half a mile east and west. It was about eighty rods wide on the west side, running this width to the east a little over half way, and it was forty or fifty rods wide on the east line. It contained about sixty acres mostly logged and cleared off, but a few logs remained lying on some of it.

We had burned the wood all up on the ground, as there was no market for it, it was worthless. We burned up out of our way enough timber to have made five thousand cords of cordwood. Father's big ax, which he brought from the State of New York, and mine, by striking innumerable blows, had been worn out long before this strip was cleared. The heavy, resounding blows of those axes had been heard, and before them many trees had fallen. They stood before the blows and trembled and swayed to and fro and at last fell with a thundering crash, to the earth, to rise no more. Some of their bodies broken, their limbs broken off, wounded and bruised, and stripped of their beautiful foliage. The noise of their fall and the force with which they struck the earth made the ground tremble and shake, and let the neighbors know that father and I were chopping, and that we were slaying the timber.

The grand old forest was melting away. The sides of many a tree had been cleft, and the chips bursted out, and they had disappeared all but their stumps. The timber was tall, I cut one whitewood that was about a foot through at the butt, and measured eighty-three feet to a limb. It ran up as straight as a liberty pole. I think our large timber was about one hundred feet high. It was, to me, a little singular that the smaller timber should run up so tall, equally as high as the large timber. All appeared anxious to look at the sun, bask their green tops in his rays and nestle and wave, in ruffles of green, above the high arching boughs of the trees. Once I saw them wave, arrayed in a different coat. Beautiful workmanship of nature was displayed in the growth of that timber.

It is not always necessary to peer through glass slides in order to take a panoramic view of the brilliant scenes dame nature presents, her varying pictures and beautiful face. Her handiwork as exhibited by herself is the most enchanting. Sometimes, the spectacle after a storm of rain and sleet is grand and sublime, but the effect of such a storm is not often seen as we view it now.

Early one spring, after nature had covered her face with a mantle of snow and appeared to repose, she aroused from her winter slumber, and adorned herself in a silvery robe. It was formed by drops of cold rain showered down upon the little snow that was left, upon the trees and, in fact, upon everything not under cover. Every bush and little twig was loaded and hung down its head. The bodies and limbs of the trees were alike covered and the boughs bent down under the heavy load of icy armor. Icicles, glistening like jewels, hung from the eaves of the house, from the fence rails, and from the limbs of our little fruit trees. The currant brush, the rose bushes, the briers and prickly ash were all encased in ice. From the points and ends of all the boughs, small and large, icicles formed and hung down like tapers. To the point of each was hanging a silver-like gem which had been frozen fast while in the act of dropping.

Some of the trees were loaded so heavily that the limbs broke off and went tearing down to the earth in a heterogeneous mass. The limbs broke in pieces and their icy coat and icicles broke up like glass.

The next morning the "Whirl-dance of the blinding storm" of sleet had passed away, but it had left its impression behind. There was formed a crust on the little snow left which gave it a shining coat, transparent as crystal. It was most beautiful. The sun shone clear and bright and cast his golden rays across the face of nature. The trees and tree-tops, the bushes and shrubs shone and glistened like so many thousand diamonds and the earth was dazzling to look upon. It appeared mystical as a silvery land, everything aglow and sparkling with radiant hues. The trees and earth seemed vying with each other in most charming beauty like many of earth's pictures.

It was a scene too bright and strange to last. A change was soon caused by the warming rays of the sun. The icicles, which hung down like jewels, melted, let go their hold and fell to the earth. The icy covering of the trees began to melt and fall like tears. Very soon the snow and ice were all gone and the ground left bare. Father said that he thought the trees were more beautiful when clothed in green leaves than when covered with ice though they were ever so bright. But to the clearing again.

Now finally I thought we had quite a clearing. I could stand by our house, and look to the west, and see Mr. Pardee's house and the smoke of his chimney. I could see Mr. Pardee and his sons when they came out in the morning and went to their work. I could look to the east and there, joining ours, was the clearing and house of Mr. Asa Blare, and he could be seen. Then it began to seem as if others were living in Michigan, for we could see them. The light of civilization began to dawn upon us. We had cleared up what was a few years before, the lair of the wolf and the hunting ground of the red man. The Michigan bird of the night had no more chance to make his nest in hollow trees or live there, but had to go back to the woods. There we could hear him almost any evening hallooing. "Whoo! whoo! whoo!" His nearest neighbor would answer him, "Whoo! whoo!" then they would get together and have a great talk about something. Whether they were talking about our chickens, or our clearing off their woods and driving them away, or something else, I cannot say as I did not understand what they said.

Father said: "Now our best wood is worth something, as the road," which is now the Michigan Central Railroad, "has got as far as Dearborn, and they are building it farther west." He thought we could cut some of our best timber into cord wood and sell it to the managers of the road, and make something from it. We drew some of the first cord wood that they used on the railroad, and continued to furnish a share of it for years. We had learned what day the first steam car was expected out to Dearborn. I went to see it, as it was to be there at a certain time of day. I was in time and with others waited anxiously for its appearance. While we were waiting I heard that there was to be a race from Mr. Conrad TenEyck's, a distance of one mile, to Dearborn. William Cremer, a young man who lived at TenEyck's, had made up his mind to have the race on his own hook and let the people of Dearborn see him come in. He got his sorrel, white-faced pony, had him saddled and bridled, and waited in readiness, so that when the iron horse came opposite he could try him a race to Dearborn, and likewise try the speed of his pony. I don't suppose the railroad men knew any thing about his arrangement. As the TenEyck tavern, where he started, stood within twenty rods of the railroad, no doubt some of the railroad men saw him when he started. Toward the village the roads ran nearer and nearer together for about a hundred rods, then came side by side for a short distance. As he had a little the start, and came to the narrows first, he must have been in plain sight of the men on the cars. It is easy to imagine how the puffs of the iron horse scared the little sorrel and gave him, if possible, more speed. The passengers who saw him might have thought it was another "train band captain, John Gilpin," running after his wife. Nearly all the people of Dearborn (who were but few at that time), had gathered in front of the arsenal, in the Chicago road, at the side of the Dearborn House and were anxiously waiting. From this point we could see half a mile down the Chicago road east, and we could see the smoke of the engine beyond the TenEyck place ...

The time appointed was up and we were very impatient, waiting and looking, for the least sign of the approach of the long-talked-of cars. As we were waiting some one said the cars would stop for Mr. TenEyck, as he was the richest and most influential man there was in the town, and the road ran a long way through his farm. Some said, "of course they will stop and take him on." At last we could hear a distant rumbling like the sound of a thousand horses running away, and we saw the smoke. As they came nearer we saw a long string of smoke disappearing in the air. The cars were approaching us rapidly, and stopped for no one. When they got opposite Mr. Thompson's tavern, sure enough, there on the Chicago road came William Cremer, like a streak, with his hat off, waving it in his hand, looking back over his shoulder at the cars, hallooing like a trooper and his horse running for dear life. He had beat them for the mile. Of course, before Cremer got up to us, we all started for the railroad, which was about twenty-five rods to the south, to see the iron horse come in. He came prancing and pawing upon the iron track, and he disdained to touch the ground. His body was as round as a log. His bones were made of iron, his veins were filled with heat, his sinews were of brass, and "every time he breathed he snorted fire and smoke." He moved proudly up to the station, little thinking that he had just been beaten by a Dearborn horse. "With his iron reins" he was easily controlled and held in subjection by his master. His groom pampered and petted him, rubbed him down, oiled his iron joints and gave him water to drink. He fed him upon the best of cord-wood, as he relished that very well, and devoured it greedily. The contents of his iron stomach seemed to be composed of fire. While he was waiting he seemed to be very impatient, letting off and wasting his breath and seeming eager for a start. He was sweating profusely. The sweat was falling in drops to the ground. When all was ready, the cry was, "All aboard!" and away he went snorting at every jump.

I went home and told the wonderful story of the sight I had seen. There was but little talked about, at our house, except the cars, until the whole family had been to see them. We thought, surely, a new era had dawned upon us, and that Michigan was getting to be quite a country.

CHAPTER XIX.

TREES.

There were two stately trees which stood near the center of the place. In view of their antiquity it seemed almost wrong to cut them. One was an elm which stood on the flat of the Ecorse. The other was what we called a swamp white oak. It stood in a little hollow at the west end of the ridge (where we lived) about twenty rods north of the elm. They appeared as though they were about the same age. They were nearly the same size. They were five or six feet through at the butt.

Father often said that the tree recorded within itself a true record of its own age. After a tree was cut down, I have known him frequently to count the grains or yearly rings and from them extract a register by which he learned how many years old it was.

How my mind reaches back forty years and views again that venerable old oak and elm. Trees whose history and lives began before the first settlement of America. How familiar still their appearance to me, as they stood with their arms stretched out bidding me the most graceful salutations. They seemed almost like friends, at least there was some companionship about them, their forms were very familiar to me.

On the west side of the elm, just above the ground and running up about six feet, there was a huge knot which grew out of the side of the tree. It was large enough to stand upon, when upon it, but there was not room enough for us to stand upon it and chop. We had to build a scaffold around the tree, up even with the top of the knot to stand upon. In that way we were able to cut the great tree down. It was a hard job and was attended with danger. When the tree started we had to get down very quickly and run back to a place of safety, for the tree was very angry in the last throes of its dissolution. It broke other trees down, tore other trees to pieces, broke off their limbs, bent other small ones down with it as it went, and held their tops to the earth. Other trees went nearly down with it but were fortunate enough to break its hold and gained again their equilibrium with such swiftness that their limbs which had been nearly broken off, yet, which they retained until they straightened, then their stopping so suddenly, the reaction caused the fractured and dry limbs to break loose, and they flew back of where we had been chopping. They flew like missiles of death through the air, and the scaffold upon which we stood but a minute before was smashed into slivers. In the mean time we were looking out for our own safety.

No man, unless he has experienced it himself, can have an adequate idea of the danger and labor of clearing a farm in heavy, timbered land. Then he knows something of the anxieties and hardships of a life in the woods: the walking, the chopping and sweating, the running and the dodging like Indians behind trees. He trusts to their protection to save him from falling trees and flying limbs, although he is often lacerated and bruised, jambed and torn by them. I knew a man and a boy in our town who were killed by falling limbs. Sometimes he is cut by the ax and is obliged to go home, over logs, between stumps and through brush, leaving a bloody trail behind him.

Father's farm was rescued from the wilderness and consecrated to the plow and husbandry through sweat and blood. We ofttimes encountered perils and were weary from labor, often times hungry and thirsty, often suffered from cold and heat, frequently destitute of comfortable apparel and condemned to toil as the universal doom of humanity—thus earning our bread by the sweat of our brows.

Father and I labored some years in sight of the great elm stump. It appeared like a giant, with a great hump on his back, overlooking the surrounding stumps. It was about eight feet high. But it was doomed to decay, and entirely disappeared long years ago.

The oak tree was more fortunate and escaped the fatal ax, a number of years after all the timber around it had been chopped and cleared away. On account of its greatness, and its having so nice a body, father let it stand as monarch of the clearing. But few came into our clearing without seeing his majesty's presence. His roots were immense. They had been centuries creeping and feeling their way along, extracting life from mother earth to sustain their gigantic body. The acorn, from which that oak grew, must have been planted long before, and the tree which grew from it have been dressed many times in its summer robe of green, and it was, doubtless, flourishing when the "Mayflower" left the English Channel. When she was slowly making her way from billow to billow, through the then almost unknown sea, bearing some of the most brave and liberty-loving men and women the world, at that time, could produce; when the hearts of the Pilgrim Fathers were beating high with hopes of liberty and escape from tyranny, when their breath came low and short for fear of what might await them; when they landed on the American shore—yes! when that little band of pilgrims were kneeling on Plymouth Rock, and offering up thanksgiving and praise to the Almighty, who had brought them safely o'er the trackless deep, that oak was quietly standing, gathering strength to make it what it was when we came to Michigan. There it had stood, ever since the days of yore, spreading its boughs over the generations of men who have long since passed away. Around it had been the Indian's camping and hunting ground. When we came to plow and work the ground near it I found some of their stone arrows which had been worked out very beautifully. Their edges and points showed very plainly where they had been chipped off in making. We also found stone hatchets, the bits of which were about two and a half inches broad and worked to an edge. They were about six inches long. The pole or head was round. From their appearance they must have been held in the hand using the arm for a helve. For an encounter with bruin or any other enemy, it is possible they bound a withe around the pole and used that as a handle. Much ingenuity and skill must have been required to work out their implements when they had nothing better with which to do it than other stones.

I often picked up the arrows and hatchets and saved them as relics of past ages, knowing that they had been in other hands long years before. I have some of them now (1875). The stones from which they were made must have been brought from some distance as there were few other stones found in this part of the country.

If that oak could have talked, what a wild, wild story it might have told, not only of lost arrows and hatchets, but also of their owners, about whom the world has little knowledge. It might have told also of the hundreds of years it had stood there and showered down its acorns upon the earth, enough in one season to have planted a forest of its own kind; how often its acorns had been gathered by the Indian youth, and devoured by the wild beasts of the forest; how many times its leaves had been changed by the autumn frosts from a green to a beautiful golden hue; how the cold wind swept them off and they flew down in huddled races to the ground, carpeted and cushioned the earth, protected the roots and enriched the soil. How, after it had been shorn of its leaves, its life current had been sent back through the pores of its body to its roots and congealed by the cold freezing frosts of winter; how the wind sighed and moaned through its branches while it cracked and snapped with the frost. But there was to be an end to its existence. The remorseless ax was laid at its roots and there is nothing left of it, unless it be a few old oak rails. There are some moss-covered rails on the place yet that were made at an early day. How my thoughts go back and linger round that oak whose branches gave shelter to the deer, furnished them with food, protected the Indian and his home—the place where I, so long afterward, advanced to manhood.

It is no wonder that Boston men are so careful in protecting their trees. With their usual care and foresight they have guarded the celebrated elm on Boston common. Thousands of the American people from every State in the Union, even from the Pacific coast, visit the beautiful city of Boston but are not satisfied until they visit the ancient elm, read its history, as far as known, from the iron plate, and gaze with admiration on the wonderful tree and the fence that surrounds it.

The full history of that tree is not known, but it reaches back prior to the settlement of Boston. It was a good sized tree in 1656. "A map of Boston made in 1722 showed the tree as one of the principal objects." That tree is a sacred relic of the past. Its branches waved over the heads of honored colonial ancestors.

Trees are our most beautiful and best antiquities. "It was a beautiful thought," says Ruskin, "when God thought of making a tree and giving it a life so long." Another says: "What vicissitudes mark its life, almost tender with suggestion. Trees are the Methuselahs of nature. The famous Etna chestnut is a thousand years old. There is a cypress tree in Mexico, over forty feet in diameter, whose zones record nearly three thousand years. The baobab trees of the Green Cape are fully four thousand years old. The great dragon tree at Ortova, Teneriffe, (recently said to be dying), is said to be five thousand years old—a life that runs parallel to almost the entire period of human chronology." No doubt some of those trees will last as long as time. Is it any wonder that I claim some companionship to trees, since I passed so many years of my youth among them? Trees often prevented sharp eyes from seeing me, secreted me and helped me to luck, which was very gratifying to me. Trees, when it rained and the wind was piercing, have often protected, sheltered and kept me dry and comfortable for hours.

I frequently when at some distance from home, hunting, and night coming on, began traveling, as I supposed, toward home. I often came to tracks in the snow which, at first, I thought were made by some one else, but, upon a more particular examination, would find that they were my own tracks. Then I would know that I had been circling round and round, that the "wigwam was lost" and I had the gloomy prospect of remaining in the woods all night—"out of humanity's reach." Then I would trust to the trees, look at them, take their directions and start again in a new course. This would seem wrong to me, but I always came out right. Trees never deceived, but showed me the way home.

When I have been in the woods, hungry, trees furnished me food. When thirsty, they often supplied me with drink. When cold and almost freezing, trees have warmed and made me comfortable. Trees furnished most of the material for father's "bark-covered house," which sheltered us for more than two years.

If trees have done so much for one, surely all humanity have derived great good from them. The earth itself is adorned and beautified by trees.

CHAPTER XX.

DRAWING CORD-WOOD—
HOW THE RAILROAD WAS BUILT—
THE STEAM WHISTLE.

Father commenced chopping cord-wood and he said I could draw it as fast as he could chop it. I was so much engaged that, when the moon was in its full, I often started with my load of wood a little before plain daylight. Of course I felt cheerful, I thought we were doing some business. Sometimes I walked by the side of the team and load and sometimes behind them. Hallooing at my team, driving them, singing, whistling and looking into the woods occasionally, occupied my time until I got to Dearbornville.

One morning I met William Ozee. I told him I had seen two or three deer as I was coming along. Told him where they stood and looked at me and the team, until we were out of sight, and that I thought they were there yet. He said he would attend to them. He had his rifle on his shoulder, and he said he would go for them. I saw him afterward and he said he had taught them better than to stand and look at anybody so impudently as that. He had killed some of them.

I made up my mind that if I could get a good rifle, I could make as much, or more, with it than father and I both could make cutting and drawing wood. Father said I might have a new one made. Accordingly I went to John W. Alexander and selected a rifle barrel, from a pack of new barrels that he had. I tried to select as soft a one as I could, as I considered those the best in frosty weather. I selected what I thought was about the right calibre, and told him I wanted him to make it with a raised sight so I could shoot any distance. I told him to make a buster for me, one that couldn't be beat. He said he would try and do it for twenty dollars. I told him I wanted him to make it as quickly as he could; in a short time he had it done. I thought it was a beautiful rifle. The name of the maker was inscribed on the barrel. I took it home feeling very good. I tried it shooting at a mark; shooting the distance of ten rods at a mark the size of a two shilling silver piece. With a rest, when there was not much wind, I could hit it every time and did do it five or six times in succession. Frequently when shooting the bullet holes would break into one another, and sometimes two bullets would go into the same hole. The only way I could tell where the last shot struck was by plugging up the old holes. Often the little white paper would fly away, the pin in the center having been shot away.

I made up my mind I had a splendid rifle, one that it would be hard to beat. That same rifle now stands in my bedroom. It was made over thirty-five years ago, with the bright name of John W. Alexander on it. He is now an old resident of Dearborn, a useful and ingenious man, and fills a prominent place in society; if he were gone it would be difficult to find a man capable of filling his place.

But I must return to my drawing wood. The place where we heaped it was on the north side of the railroad, about fifteen rods east of where the postoffice is now kept. The woodyard, including the depot, I should judge, was not more than one hundred feet square. Here we piled our wood, sometimes ten feet high. We were to have seven shillings a cord for it and if we chopped and hauled three cords a day we thought we did well. I drew it as fast as I could, sometimes I got to Dearborn just as the old Solar made his appearance in the east. The Lunar had already done her work toward helping me, veiled her face and disappeared. When we had drawn a lot of wood in father had it measured up and got his voucher for the amount. One time when he went to Detroit to get his money I went with him. We went on the cars. The depot and railroad office, where father did his business, stood where the City Hall now stands. I thought the railroad was a splendid thing. We went in so much nicer, easier and quicker than we could have gone on foot, or with our ox-team.

Now we were going to get some money of the railroad officers, I thought we would have money to pay the interest on our mortgage and help us along. Father got his pay in Michigan State scrip, a substitute for money. It was good for its face to pay State taxes; but to turn it into money father had to sell it for six shillings on a dollar. Here it will be seen, that what we really received for our wood, was a little over sixty-five cents per cord, and that when we drew in three cords a day (which was as much as father could chop, and all that I and the team could draw) we made a little over a dollar and ninety-five cents per day.

What would some of the workingmen of the present day who get together and form "Union Leagues," "Trade Unions," strike for higher wages and conspire against their employers and their capital, doubtless thinking such a course justifiable, think of such wages as that, and provisions very dear, as they were at that time? I began to think myself rough and ready and was able to grapple with almost anything and do a good days' work. Father, I and the team all worked hard and with the wood thrown in we all together did not make two dollars a day.

As father had a small job in the building of the railroad and some of the time I was with him, I will describe as well as I can, how the railroad was built. They first graded the road-bed and made it level, then took timbers as long as the trees would make them, hewed them on each side and flattened them down to about a foot in thickness, then laid them on blocks which were placed in the bed of the road. They were laid lengthwise of the road, far enough apart so that they would be directly under the wheels of the cars, and the ground graded up around them. In this manner they continued until the road-bed was finished.

The next thing was to get out the ties. These were made from logs nine feet long, which were split open through the heart, then quartered and split from the heart to the center of the back, until the pieces were about six or seven inches through on the back. Then the backs of the ties were hewed flat, making them about three square, when they were ready to be used on the road. They were placed back down across the bed pieces and spiked fast to them. They were laid about three feet apart the length of the road. Over those sills, in the upper edge of the ties, they cut out two gains. In those gains they laid two stringers running directly over the sleepers. These stringers were sawed out about four by six inches square. They were laid in the gains of the ties, spiked fast and wedged with wooden wedges. Then the woodwork was finished and everything ready for pulling on the iron. They used the strap rail iron. The bars were two inches and a quarter wide and half an inch thick. These bars were laid flat on top, and next to the in-edge, of the stringers and were spiked fast to them. In this way our railroad was built. The cars running away west on it, penetrating Michigan as the harbinger of civilization, opened up a way for the resources of the country.

The strap iron which they used first proved to be very poor iron. In after years, if a spike came out or the bar cracked off at the spike hole, the bar would turn up like a serpent's head and if not seen in time it was liable to throw the train off the track and do damage. I was at Dearborn at one time when an accident, of this kind, happened to a freight train, a little west of the village. There was considerable property destroyed, barrels broken in pieces and flour strewed over the ground, but no lives were lost.

Father said the railroad was a good thing for us and our country, and that they would soon have one, and the cars running on it to the State of New York. Then I reiterated my promise to mother. I said if the cars ran through our native place, we could go back there without crossing Lake Erie, the thought of which chilled me every time I spoke to mother about going back to make a visit. Time sped on, days, months, and some years had passed, since the first of the Michigan Central Railroad was built, and the cars running east and west loaded with passengers and freight, when one morning I heard a strange noise. It was terrible and unaccountable to me, as much so as it would have been if I had heard heavy thunder at mid-day, from a clear sky. I heard it from the direction of Dearbornville; It appeared to originate there, or in the woods that way. I heard it two or three times, several days in succession.

If there had come a herald from Dearbornville and told me that the man of the moon had stepped out of his old home, and down on to our earth, at Dearborn, and that he had a great horn, twenty feet long, in his hand, and that it was him, I had heard, tooting on his horn to let us know, and the inhabitants of his own country, that he had arrived safe on the earth, I might not have believed what he said in regard to the arrival of the supernatural being and his visit to us; but I could have believed almost anything wonderful in regard to the horn for I had heard its thrilling blast myself.

Father, mother and, in fact, none of us were able to think or imagine what it could be. It came through the woods as swift as lightning and its shrill and piercing voice was more startling than thunder. It echoed and re-echoed across our clearing, from woods to woods and died swiftly away in the distance. What on earth could it be? Could it be the voice of a wild animal? That seemed impossible, it was too loud. I thought such an animal would need lungs as large as a blacksmith's bellows, and a voice as strong as a steamboat, to have raised such an unearthly yell.

It was enough to scare all the bears and wolves to death, or at least, enough to make them hide away from the voice and face of the dragon. But there was a man, who lived one mile south of Dearbornville, by the name of Alonzo Mather; he was a little more sensible and courageous. He thought he knew what made the strange noise. When he came out of his house one morning, all at once, the terrible sound broke upon his ear. He had heard it two or three times before, about the same place in the woods, toward Dearbornville. He said to his hired man, a Mr. Whitmore, who was utterly astonished and seemed to be all in a fright, "Hear that! I know what it is! It is a bear, and he lives right over there in the woods.

I have heard him two or three times in the same place. Don't say a word to anyone; not let the hunters know anything about his being there and I'll shoot him myself.'" He took down his rifle immediately, and started on the double quick, followed by the hired man, who could help him in case of trouble.

He went through the woods looking carefully in every direction, scanning the old logs and large hollow trees and searching from top to bottom to see if he could find a hole large enough for a bear to crawl in. In this way he looked all around, near the railroad, where he thought the noise originated, but he could not find a track or sign of Mr. Bruin, for the bear wasn't there, so, in disgust, he gave up the hunt.

About the next day after Mr. Mather's hunt, he and all the rest of us learned what had caused the excitement. It was a new invention, the steam whistle of the cars; something we had never heard before.

CHAPTER XXI.

HOW I HUNTED AND WE PAID THE MORTGAGE.

The mortgage which had hung so long over us, like a dark cloud obscuring our temporal horizon and chilling our hopes, was at last removed, May first, 1841. After the mortgage was on the place it hardly seemed to me as if it were ours. It was becoming more and more valuable all the time, and I thought it was dangerous to let the mortgage run, as the old lady might foreclose at any time and make us trouble and expense. The mortgage was like a cancer eating up our substance, gnawing day and night as it had for years. I made up my mind it must be paid. I knew it caused mother much trouble and although, father said very little about it, I knew that he would be over-joyed to have it settled up. I told him I thought I had better hunt during one fall and winter and that I thought I could, in that way, help him raise money to pay the mortgage. I was about twenty years old at that time and thought I had a very good rifle and knew how to use it.

I went to my friend William Beal, and told him I had concluded to hunt through the winter. I asked him if he didn't want to join with me and we would hunt together, at least some of the time. He said he would. I told him I thought we could make more money by hunting than we could in any other way as deer were worth, on an average, from two and a half to five dollars a piece at Detroit, and we could take them in very handily on the cars.

We found the deer very numerous in the town of Taylor, next south of the town of Dearborn. Sometimes we went and stayed a week. We stopped nights with an old gentleman whose name was Hodge. He always appeared very glad to see us and gave us a hearty welcome. As he and his old lady (at that time) lived alone, no doubt they were glad of our company. They must have felt lonesome and they knew they would be well rewarded with venison and money for the trouble we made them. Mrs. Hodge took as much pains for us and used us as well as mother could have done. We carried our provisions there on our backs, flour, potatoes, pork and whatever we needed. We carried pork for the reason we relished it better a part of the time than we did venison. Mrs. Hodge prepared our meals at any time we wanted them. Sometimes we ate our breakfast before daylight and were a mile or two on the runway of the deer when in became light. The woods and oak openings abounded in deer and we had very good luck as a general thing. We made it a rule to stay and not go home until we had killed a load, which was not less than six. Then we went and got father's oxen and sled to go after and bring them home. After we brought them home we took the hind quarters, the hide, and sometimes whole deer, to Detroit and sold them. In this way we got considerable money. In fact my pocket-book began to pod out a little. Of course, we saved enough, of the fore-quarters for our family use and for our old friends, Mr. and Mrs. Hodge. But we couldn't afford to let them have the saddles; we wanted them to sell as we were going in for making money.

It would be impossible for me to delineate the occurrences incident to my hunting days. The story told in full would fill a volume, but if it were not in connection with my father's family and how we got along, when I was at home with him, I should not mention it at all. As it is, I will try to describe one day's hunt after deer, which might be called a successful day, and another hunt after bears, which was not successful and one or two deer fights. My comrade and I started from father's very early one morning. A nice tracking snow, three or four inches deep, had fallen during the fore part of the night. In the morning it was warm and pleasant. When we came near the head of the windfall, we found the tracks where three large bucks had been along. It is not common that those large deer go together. They are generally scattering, one or two, or with other deer, but in this case, it seemed, three old bucks had agreed to go together. We followed them about half a mile to the west until they crossed what is now the old telegraph road in the town of Taylor, south of where Mr. Putnam lives. We thought the deer went into a large thicket, that stands there yet. We made up our minds they were lying in that thicket. William said he would go around and stand on the ridge, beyond the thicket, in a good place to see them when they were driven out. I told him I wanted him to be sure and down with one, so that I could see how they looked. I stood where he left me about half an hour, to give him plenty of time to get around, then I started along slow on the tracks.

I followed them about ten or fifteen rods when I found, that instead of going into the thicket where we supposed, they had turned into a little thicket, near a fence and clearing that had been made at an early day. I little thought they were lying there, but sure enough, in a minute, they jumped up and away they went, one after the other, toward the big thicket. They seemed desirous of making all the sport of me they could; as they were running across a little opening they showed me their white flags. I shot very quickly at the middle one. I told him by the report of my rifle, which rang out clear on the morning air, that I wanted him to stop, and he struck his flag.

They were running from me a little diagonally, and were about twenty-five rods off, when my bullet struck his side, it being partly toward me. They ran right into the big thicket where we first supposed they lay. I loaded my rifle and went where they were running when I shot. I saw that the blood flew in small particles on the snow and I was sure he was ours. He ran for one breath, got out of my sight and fell dead, having made his last tracks, being shot through the lights.

I hurried across to my friend Beal and told him I had shot a noble buck. That he was running away from me and that I would not allow him to do so. The other two had gone out of the thicket, over the ridge, so far east that he didn't see them at all. We hurried back to where the one we had got lay, took out his entrails, climbed up a sapling, bent down the top and fastened the gambrels of the old buck to it; then sprinkled powder on his hair, so as to keep the ravens from picking him, let go the sapling and it straightened up with him so that he was out of the way of the dogs and wolves. Then we started as quickly as possible after the other two. They went a south-west direction about eighty rods, then turned south-east and went straight for the Indian hill, went over it and took their course nearly east. They had ceased to run and were walking. There was another large thicket east of us, which was about half a mile through and we thought, possibly, they might stop in that before they went through into the woods. It was agreed that I should go around, that time, to the lower end of the thicket, and stand. He was to try and drive them through if they were there. I went south to, what we called, the south branch of the Reed creek. It was frozen over and there were three or four inches of snow on the ice; I went on it without making any noise. I ran down a little over half a mile very quickly; when I was below the thicket I turned north, went through the brush that grew on the bank of the creek, up to a little ridge where it was open and stopped by the side of a tree, which was about twenty or thirty rods from where I turned north.

I didn't stand there but a very short time before I heard and saw some partridges fly away, and I knew they had been disturbed by something in the thicket. Then I saw the two deer coming just as straight toward me as they could run, one right after the other. When they got within about eight or ten rods of me I had my rifle ready. They saw me and, as they went to jump side-wise, my rifle spoke to another one and the voice of it forbade him going any farther. That was the second word my rifle had spoken that morning.

The deer turned and ran in a semi-circle half round me in plain sight, then off, out of sight, over the ridge where Doctor Snow's farmhouse now stands, in the town of Taylor. In a few moments out came my comrade; I asked him, what the report of my rifle said, as it burst through the thicket by him and echoed over the Indian hill. He said he thought it spoke of luck. We followed the old buck a little ways over the ridge and came to where he had made his last jump. He was a beautiful fellow, equally as fine as the first one.

Then we thought we had done well enough for one day, we had each of us one. So we cut a wooden hook, put it into his under-jaw, both took hold and drew him up where the other one hung. We put them together and started slowly for home. We were following along an old trail and had drawn both deer about half a mile together, when we came to where five or six deer had just crossed. They were going south-east and we were going north-east. While we were looking at the tracks two men came in sight. One was Mr. Arvin Sheldon, the other Mr. Holdin. We knew them very well and knew that they were good hunters. They looked at our deer and said that we must hang them up, said they would help us. So we bent down two saplings and hung the deer up, side by side, then we started with them. It was early in the day, perhaps about ten o'clock. We followed the deer beyond what is now Taylor Center, and into the west woods two miles from there. Near Taylor Center, Holdin left us. He thought there were too many of us together, and went off to try his luck alone and followed another flock. We found that these deer were very shy and it seemed impossible for us to get a shot at them.

After we got into the west woods we were bound to stick to the same ones. It was late in the afternoon and as we were getting so far from home, we thought we had better use a little stratagem. We would go very slowly; it was agreed that I should follow the tracks and that the other two should be governed by my movements. One was to go to my right, and keep as far off as he could and see me, through the woods; he was to keep a little ahead of me. The other was to manage in the same way at my left. When we started we were something in the shape of a letter V, only spread more. If I went fast they were to go fast and if I went slowly they were to do the same. They were to watch me and look out ahead for the deer. We traveled some little distance in this way when I saw a deer standing about thirty-five rods off. It was a long shot, but I drew up my rifle and fired. Mr. Sheldon had two clogs with him and when I shot they broke from him and ran after the deer we had been following. They went yelling after them, out of hearing. It was always my practice, after I shot, to stand in my tracks and load my rifle, keeping my eye on the place where the deer were. When I shot, my comrades started for me and soon we three friends were together. Sheldon remarked, that he guessed I hadn't hit that one. I asked him why. He said the dogs had already gone out of hearing and that if I had killed one, they would have stopped. I left the tracks and walked along in the direction of where the deer had stood, watching upon the snow and brush to see if I could see any signs where the bullet had struck a bush or twig, until I came to the place where the deer had stood. It proved to be, not one of those we had been following, but an old buck that had just got up out of the bed where he had been lying and was standing over it when I fired. I looked and saw some short hair lying on the snow, and told Mr. Sheldon that that looked as if I had made a square shot and that the dogs had gone after the well ones we had been following, that this one was an old buck which we hadn't disturbed before. I thought perhaps he had got up to see the flock that we were following go by. We didn't follow him more than ten rods before we found where he lay last. He was a very large buck, a full mate for either of those we already had.

A little ways back we had crossed a coon's track and we knew that he had been along in the latter part of the night, as it snowed in the earlier part of the night. We thought he hadn't gone far, so we agreed that Sheldon should follow his tracks and find his tree, (at that time coon skins were valuable) while we went back about a mile, to a lone settler's, by the name of Plaster, (who lived on the openings) and borrowed an ax. When we came back to the woods we were to halloo and he was to answer us. We had to do what we did very quickly as it was getting near night. When we had borrowed the ax and were nearly back to the woods again, we heard the report of Sheldon's rifle, as it rang out of the timber clear and sharp and died away in the oak openings. When we got into the woods we hallooed for him, he answered and we went to him; he had found the tree. We asked him what he had shot at, he said at a deer, but missed him. We cut down the tree and were rewarded by getting four coons. Afterward I sold the coon skins in Detroit for a dollar apiece. That Mr. Arvin Sheldon is now an old resident of the town of Taylor and lives about two miles south-west of me.

After we got the tree cut down and the coons secure, it was between sundown and dark. We were six or seven miles from home and then had to take the ax home. Late that evening, when I got back under the old paternal roof, there was one there who was very tired but the excitement of the day helped him a little. By hunting (and it was hard work for me as I made a business of it) I accumulated a considerable sum of money. Father had earned and saved some money, so that with what I had, he made out enough to pay off the mortgage to Mrs. Phlihaven and had it cancelled. Then his farm was clear. If I had not felt anxious about it myself, the joy expressed by the other members of the family, when they knew that the mortgage was paid, would have been a sufficient reward for all the labors I had performed, for all the weary walks, the running and racing done, while upon the chase, both day and night.

It is a little singular that an animal as mild and harmless as the deer ordinarily is, should when cornered or wounded have such courage that he will fight man or dog in his own defense, jumping upon them, striking with his feet. As their hoofs are sharp they cut to the quick, at the same time they are hooking with their horns. I will relate one or two incidents. One of which came under my own observation:

I was out hunting with R. Crandell. We were near the Reed creek when he shot a buck. The deer fell. Crandell thought he was sure of him; handed his rifle to me. I told him to stand still and load his gun, but he ran like an Indian; he took long steps. When he got up near, the old buck had gotten a little over the shock the bullet gave him and he got up, turned upon Crandell, raised the hair upon his back so that it stood forward. Then the scene changed; Crandell ran, and the deer ran after him. He came very near catching Crandell and must have done so if he had not dodged behind a tree, and around it he went and the deer after him. Crandell said he called upon his legs to be true to his body then if ever; and I thought, judging from the way those members of his organism were carrying him around that tree, that they were exerting every nerve to save him. He hallooed every minute for me to shoot the deer. But the race was so amusing, I did not care to hurry having never seen such an exhibition of Crandell's speed before. (Without doubt he did his level best). Soon, however, I thought it necessary and I shot the deer. Crandell said I had laughed enough to kill myself. He appeared to be displeased with me; said I was too slow, and might have released him quicker.

Some two or three years after this, Crandell had another hunt with a Mr. Holden, of Dearbornville. The incidents of which are given in his own words: "Being anxious for a hunt, Holden and myself started out for a deer hunt on our southern hunting ground. After traveling about three-fourths of a mile from Dearbornville, Holden, being a little way from me, started a buck, he running directly south; I told Holden where to go on a certain road, newly cut out, and stand and I would drive the deer to him from the east. As expected, I soon started him and Holden's dog followed the deer straight to him. In about three minutes whang went Holden's gun; I ran with all my might. The dog had stopped barking and I knew the deer was ours. But, when I got to the road, I heard Holden hallooing loudly for help. The deer had jumped across the road into the old tree tops and the dog caught him. Holden saw that the deer was getting the better of the dog, laid down his gun, took out his knife and went for the deer. When he got up to the deer the deer paid all his attention to him instead of the dog. The deer had gotten Holden down between two logs and stood on him, stamping and hooking him desperately. Holden said: 'For God sake kill him or he will kill me.'

"I was so much excited I was afraid to shoot for fear of killing Holden or the dog, but I shot and the deer fell lengthwise on Holden, I rolled him off and Holden got up, all covered with blood from head to foot, with his clothes torn into shreds. He looked at himself and said despondingly, 'What a spectacle I am!' I peeled some bark, tied his rags round him, patched him up the best possible and we started for home through the woods, got as near his home as we could and not be seen, then I left him, went to his house and got him some clothes, took them back to him and helped him put them on. When clothed he went home a bruised and lacerated man."

CHAPTER XXII.

BEAR HUNT OF 1842.

One day in winter my brother-in-law, Reuben Crandell, and myself started to go hunting deer, as we supposed. We went south across the windfall, started a flock of deer and were following them. We had a good tracking snow and thought it was a good day for hunting. We followed the deer south across Reed Creek and saw a little ahead of us quite a path. It appeared as though a herd of ponies had passed along there. (Then there were plenty of French ponies running in the woods.) When we came up to the trail or path, that we saw they had made, in the snow we discovered it was four bears which had made the path. They had passed along a little time before for their tracks were fresh and new. There seemed to be a grand chance for us and we started after them. We either walked very fast or ran, sometimes as fast as we could stand it to run.

In this way we had followed them several miles and expected to see them every minute. We were going a little slower when I looked one side of us and there was an Indian, on a trot, going in the same direction that we were. I told Crandell that he had seen our tracks and knew that we were after the bears and that he was trying to cut us off and get the bears away from us. Just then I saw the bears and drew up my rifle and shot at one, as he was standing on an old log. The Indian then turned and ran up to the bear tracks to see, probably, if I had killed one. I told Crandell to go on with him and not let him get the start of us and I would load my rifle, as quickly as possible, and follow.

Being in a hurry, I did not place my bullet right on the patch, in the muzzle of the rifle and it bothered me in getting down. When it was loaded, I broke for them. I could just see Crandell putting in the best he could and trying to make two-forty time; but he was alone the Indian had left him. Then there might have been seen some long steps and tall running done by me, in those woods, (if any one had been there to witness it) for about eighty rods. When I came up with Crandell I asked him where the Indian was; he said, "Yonder he goes almost out of sight." I asked him what he let him get ahead for; he said that he could not keep up with him, and that he had told him, two or three times, to stop and wait for me, but he would not pay the least attention to what he said. I told him to keep on the tracks as fast as he could, and I would try to stop the Indian.

I saw that the four bears' tracks were all together yet, and Crandell said I didn't hit one when I shot. I thought it was singular and that perhaps my bullet had struck a bush or twig, glanced off and saved Mr. Bruin's hide. Now it looked as though the Indian was going to get our bears away from us, sure enough, and now for a chase that is more excitable than is often seen in the woods.

The Indian was on a good lope after the bears and I on a good run after him. I had the advantage of the Indian, the bears would run crooked. Sometimes they would run on a large log and follow it its whole length right in another direction from the way they had been going. The Indian had to follow their tracks; I followed him by sight and cut off the crooks as much as I could. In this way I ran at least half a mile after leaving Crandell and was cutting off and gaining on the Indian fast, and had got near enough to have hallooed at him and told him to stop. But I though that would do no good, that it was necessary for me to overtake him, and I was bound to stop him. I had got up to within fifteen rods and as good luck would have it, the bears turned from an easterly course around to the northwest. The Indian turned also and I struck across the elbow and came to the tracks ahead of him. I stood facing him when he came up and informed him that the bears were ours. I told him that he should not follow them another step, and to wait, right where he was, until the other man came up. I am sure the Indian thought the white man had outrun him and maybe he did not think how it was done. He stood there perfectly still, and I guard over him. I thought he looked ugly and mad; he would hardly say a word. In two or three minutes Crandell came up, puffing-and blowing like a porpoise. The sweat was running off him in profusion, and while wiping it from his brow with his hands, he said to the Indian: "You would not stop when I told you to, if I had got a good sight of you I would have shot you." Of course Crandell only said this because he wanted to scare the Indian as he had no thought of shooting, or hurting him in the least.

We started slowly off on the bear tracks and left the Indian standing and looking at us. I told Crandell I thought the Indian was scared and very mad at us for his threatening to shoot him, and my stopping him; that if he got us both in range, it might be possible he would shoot us. I told him to walk at least a rod one side of me so as not to get both in range of his rifle and I thought he would not dare to disturb us. As we walked away I would once in a while turn an eye over my shoulder and look back to see the Indian. He stood there like a statue until we were out of sight and I never saw that Indian again.

As soon as we were fairly out of sight of him we walked fast and finally tried running, some of the time as long as we could stand it. One of the bears was large, another about the common size and two were small; the small ones followed behind. They were a fine sight passing through the woods, but they led us a wild chase. Late in the afternoon they crossed the Reed Creek going north, partly in the direction of father's home. Crandell said, "Now I know where we are. I can follow up the creek until I get to the Reed house and then take the path home. I am so tired I cannot follow the bears another step." So he sat down to rest. I told him to come on, it was necessary for us to have two or three of those bears and I thought if we could kill one of the large ones the small ones would be likely to hang around until we could shoot them. But I could not get him to go another step. He said he was going home and I told him I was going to follow the bears. I went after them as fast as it was possible, and after awhile came in plain sight of them. The large one was standing with his fore feet upon a log, broadside to me and looking back at me. I thought Crandell would see how much he missed it leaving me. I drew up my rifle and fired, "ping went the rifle ball" and it made the woods ring, but away went the bears. I expected to see the bear drop, or at least roll and tumble. I loaded my rifle and went up to where Mr. Bruin had stood. I looked to see if I had not cut off some of his hair, but could see no signs of having touched him with the bullet. I followed along a little ways and made up my mind I had not hit him. I thought it strange; it was a fair broadside shot, not more than twenty or twenty-five rods off, and what the reason was I had missed him I could not tell. I followed them on, very much discouraged and miserably tired, after a little they were making almost straight for father's clearing. I followed them into the windfall within half a mile of home. It was then about sundown and as their tracks turned off I thought I would leave following them until next morning, and would then start after them again.

As I came in sight of our clearing I thought, as usual, I would fire off my rifle at a mark, which was on the side of a tree, about ten rods off; I drew it up and shot. My parents knew by the report and sharp song of my rifle that I was coming; it was my parting salute to the forest. As the sound of it penetrated the lonely gloom and died away in the darkness of the woods I looked at the mark on the tree, to see where my bullet had struck. I had shot nearly a foot right over it. Then I looked at the sight of my rifle and found that the back sight had been raised clear up. Strange to say, I had not noticed it before. No doubt it was done by one of my little sisters or John S. They must have taken it down and been fooling with it, on the sly. Then I knew the reason of my bad luck. I think a more tired and discouraged hunter than I was, never crawled out of the woods. With my, hitherto, trusty companion I had met with a signal defeat. I had carried it hundreds of miles on my shoulder and was not afraid, with it, to face anything in the woods, day or night; but this time it failed me and the bears escaped.

The report of my rifle, that evening, seemed changed as if the very sound told of my bad luck. I made up my mind, as I went into the house, that the next morning; we would raise as many men and as many dogs as there were bears and try them again. Of course I was too tired to notify any one that night myself, so John S. went down to Mr. Purdy's. I knew he had a large dog, which he called Watch, that was not afraid to tackle anything that ran in the woods, on four legs. I told J.S. to tell Mr. Purdy that I had been following a pack of bears, and that I wanted him to come early the next morning, and be sure and bring his dog to go with me after them. We had a good dog, and I sent Crandell word to be ready with his dog. James Wilson volunteered to go with us and take his dog; they were to be on hand at daylight in the morning. After we got together ready to start after the bears I told them that I thought the dogs would at least tree the small bears. We all started for the bear tracks. We took my back tracks; when we got to the tree I showed them the shot I had made the night before, and told them the reason I was not able to take one, or more, of those bears by the heels the day before, and then I might have examined them at my leisure.

We followed my tracks until we found where I left the bear tracks, then we followed them. T supposed they were so tired they would lie down and rest, probably in the windfall. But they were too badly scared for that. They seemed to have traveled all night. We followed them across the north part of the town of Taylor, through-the oak openings, into what we called the west woods and into the town of Romulus. They had given us a wide range before we came up to them, but here in a swamp or swale, between two sand ridges, we found them. They saw us first and ran. As soon as we saw we had started them we let the dogs go. They started with a rush.

"And then the dogs the game espy;
An ill bred and uncivil pack;
And such a wild discordant cry!
Another fury on his back!"

—*Bishop.*

We could hear them yelp, yelp, yelp, while they were on the tracks and heard them when they came up to the bears. Then there was a wonderful confusion of voices. We could hear our dogs and they seemed to be struggling hard for their lives. "Bow-wow, bow, bowwow, yelp, yelp, yelp, tii, tii, tii."

When the dogs got to the bears we were about half a mile from them. We hurried through the brush and over the logs, as fast as possible, to help our canine friends for we supposed that they were in a life and death struggle. It is now my opinion that there never was such a noise and conflict in those woods before, nor since, at least heard by white men. When we were about half way to where the battle raged most furiously, it was all at once still; we could not hear a sound from them any more. We went a little farther and met old Watch, and some of the other dogs crawling back. Watch, by his wounds, gave a good report of his courage himself. He was bleeding; had been wounded and torn badly. He was hurt the worst of any of the dogs. Before we reached the battle ground we met the last one; he was not hurt at all, he had kept a proper distance. But they were all badly whipped or scared. They had got enough of the bears.

"Sir Bruin to his forest flew,
With heart as light as paws were fleet;
Nor further dare the curs pursue,
It was a 'masterly retreat.'"

—*Bishop.*

When we got to the battle ground we could see where they had fought, clenched and rolled over and over. The blood of the dogs was sprinkled all around on the snow. We saw that it was the large bears which did the fighting. They would not leave the small ones but fought for them. We saw in one place, where the fight was the most severe, one bear had attempted to climb a tree. He went up a piece on one side of it and down the other, then jumped off, before we got in sight, and ran. We could see by the marks of the claws, on the bark of the tree, and the tracks, where he jumped oft, that he had climbed part way up.

I have seen hundreds of times in the woods where bears had reached up as high as they could around little trees and scratched them. It showed the plainest on beech trees as their bark is smooth. It is easy to see the size of the bear's paws and his length from the ground by these marks on the trees.

That day we saw where the bears had done some marking of dogs as well as trees. We found that the dogs had separated the bears, some having gone one way and some another. The grit had been taken out of us as well as out of the dogs, and the bear hunt had lost its charms for us. We were a long ways from home and we thought it best to get our wounded dogs back there again, if we could. We gave up the chase and let those bears go. I felt the effects of the previous day's chase and tired out more easily; I wished I had let the Indian have the bears to do what he was a mind to with, and that I had never seen them.

I presume there are now many persons in Wayne County, who little think that thirty-three years ago, 1842, there could have been four wild bears followed, in different towns in that county, for two days; yet such was the case. This was about the last of my hunting. My attention was called to other business, of more importance which I thought it was necessary for me to attend to, so I hung up my rifle and have not used it to hunt with, in the woods, six full days since. That Indian, who wanted the bears, was the last Indian I ever saw in the woods hunting for a living.

I don't think there is a wild deer in the town of Dearborn at this day and but very few, if any, in Wayne County. I heard that there was one bear killed by a man, near the mouth of the Ecorse, last fall, 1874. He was a stranger and, no doubt, far from his native home. He was the first one I have heard of being seen in this country for years.

CHAPTER XXIII.

GRANDFATHER'S POWDER-HORN—
WAR WITH PIRATES.

Time sped on. The earth had traveled its circuit many times since father sold his little place in Putnam County, State of New York, and bade adieu to all the dear scenes of his childhood and youth and came to battle, for himself and family in the wilds of Michigan. And he did his part bravely. He was a strong man; mentally and physically strong, and possessed just enough of the love of a romantic and strange life, to help him battle successfully with the incidents and privations common to such as settle in a new country, with but little capital. He worked his way through. He had a very retentive memory and possessed the faculty of pleasing his visitors, to no common extent.

Father at the close of the Tripoli war, 1805, was about the age that I was when we started for Michigan. He often told me of the war with Tripoli and trouble with Algiers. He gloried in the name of an American and often related the prowess and bravery of our soldiers, in defending their flag and the rights of American citizens, at home and abroad, on the land and on the sea.

Of course when the Fourth of July came round I went to celebrate the day. As cannon were almost always fired at Dearbornville, on that day, I would go out there to listen to the big guns and their tremendous roar, as they were fired every minute for a national salute. The sound of their booming died away beyond Detroit River, in Canada, and let the

Canadians, and all others in this part of the universe, know that we were holding the Fourth of July in Dearbornville. When I went home at night I told father about it, and what a good time I had enjoyed, and that they fired one big gun in honor of Michigan.

On such days his patriotic feelings were wrought up and he talked much of wars, patriotism and so forth. On such an occasion he told me that his father, William Nowlin, was a captain of militia, in the State of New York, when he was a boy. That I was named for him and that, when he was done with it, I should have my grandfather's ancient powder-horn. It is red and carved out very nicely, covered with beautiful scrolls and old-fashioned letters. The two first letters of my grandfather's name, W. N., are on it, and toward the smaller end of the horn—my father's given name, John. These were inscribed on it long since the horn was made. It was made when Washington was about twenty-five years old, and, no doubt, saw service in the French and Indian war, in the defence of the English colonies of America. Its history, some of it, is shrouded in mystery. It has passed down through the revolutionary war, and the war of 1812, through four generations of men, and was given to me by my father as an heir-loom, a relic of the past.

Next to my father's given name is the inscription, E.b. Then follows these old lines:

"I, powder, with my brother ball,
A hero like, do conquer all."

"'Tis best abroad with foreign foes to fight,
And not at home, to feel their hateful spite,
Where all our friends of every sex and age,
Will be expos'd unto their cruel rage."

—Lieut. Abl Prindel's. Made at No. 4. June 30th, 1757.

The letters are old fashioned, the "s" on it is made as an "f" is made now. I presume it was a present from Lieut. Prindel to grandfather. This horn is sixteen inches long, measures nine and one-half inches around the butt and would hold fully four pounds of powder.

Father said in the war with Tripoli, 1803, one of the Barbary States, Captain Bainbridge sailed, in the Philadelphia, to Tripoli and chased one of the pirate boats into the harbor. He ventured a little too far and ran aground. The officers were made prisoners and the crew slaves, to the Turks, and joined their countrymen who had preceded them. But, father said, the Americans were too brave a people to be subjected to slavery. Other Americans rescued them and it was proved that the United States would protect their flag throughout all the world. He often told me of Commodore Decatur and William Eaton. They were among his ideal American heroes. He said that Decatur conceived the idea of retaking the "Philadelphia" and destroying her. He sailed into the harbor of Tripoli at night and up to the "Philadelphia," made his vessel, the "Intrepid," fast to her side and sprang on board. There he had often walked before under very different circumstances, in the light of other days, when thousands of miles away and among his friends. Now how changed the scene! The "Philadelphia" was in an enemy's hands, and her guns loaded, to turn on her former owners at a moment's notice. Decatur was followed by seventy or eighty men, as brave Americans as ever walked on deck. The surprise was complete, and the astonished Turks now saw the decks swarming with Americans, armed and with drawn swords in their hands. Some of the Tripolitans lost their heads, some of them cried for quarters, others tried to climb in the shrouds and rigging of the ship and some jumped overboard.

In ten minutes' time, Decatur and his crew were masters of the frigate. Now what grieved him most was that the noble ship, which they had rescued from the barbarous Arabs, had to be burned, it being impossible to remove her from the sandbar where she lay. So they brought, on board the "Philadelphia," combustible material, which they had with them on the "Intrepid," and set her on fire. In a short time the flames were leaping and dancing along the sides of the doomed ship. The devouring fire, greedily burning, cracking and hissing, destroyed the timbers, leaped up the spars, caught hold of the rigging and lighted up the whole place. It could have been, and was, seen for miles. The spectacle was awfully grand as well as sublime. Tripoli was lighted up and hundreds of people could be seen in the streets, by the light of the burning ship.

The land forts and corsairs were all in plain sight of the American fleet. The light enabled the enemy to see the bold "Intrepid," with her valiant crew, leaving the burning ship and sailing away toward the American blockading fleet. The forts and some of the galleys opened fire upon them; it was one continuous roar of cannon belching forth fire and missiles of death. The balls and shot went singing over their heads and around, some striking the water and raising a cloud of spray which flew in all directions. But the victorious crew paid no attention and quietly sailed away to join their country's defenders. They were soon beyond the reach of the foe and out of danger. Then they had time to consider what they had accomplished. They had entered the enemy's stronghold, re-captured and burned the "Philadelphia" and put her Arab crew to the sword, or driven them into the sea. All this they did without the loss of a single man. Father said that the inhabitants of Tripoli were Turks who exacted taxes and received tribute from all Christian nations; that they had taken some of the American seamen and held them as slaves. The Bashaw declared war with America, (a country about which he knew but very little.) He put his American slaves in chain-gangs, in this way they were obliged to labor for that government. There was no chance for them to escape and they must remain in slavery unless rescued by their countrymen. Father said that the Turks of Tripoli were a band of pirates, in disguise, robbers upon the high seas.

The war occurred during the administration of President Jefferson. Congress sent Commodore Preble with a squadron of seven sail, and a thousand men, armed with heavy cannon. They appeared before Tripoli;

the reigning Bashaw refused to treat for peace or give up his slaves, without he received a large ransom. Then it was that the thunder of the American cannon broke upon Tripoli and the bombardment of that city commenced, 1830. They were answered by hundreds of the enemy's guns. The earth trembled, the sea shook, the wild waves danced and the white caps broke as the cannon balls glanced on, plowed their way and plunged into the water. The strong buildings of Tripoli trembled to their foundations and hundreds of Arabs, who were out upon their roofs when the battle commenced, to witness it, in five minutes' time were skedaddling for their lives. The Bashaw's castle and the entire city felt severely the heavy blows of the American cannon. The enemy's fleet took refuge under the forts and away from the ships of North America. The "Constitution" sunk one of their boats, run two aground and the rest got under shelter the best they could.

One of the last wonders of the wrath of the Americans was poured out upon Tripoli in the shape of a fire ship. It contained one hundred barrels of powder stored away below deck, in a room prepared expressly for its reception. On the deck, over the powder, was placed hundreds of shells and pieces of iron, which the powder, when it exploded, would hurl as messengers of destruction among the enemy. The "Intrepid" was the ship selected for the daring deed. She was Decatur's favorite; with her he captured the "Philadelphia." There were twelve American braves who volunteered to take the fire-ship into the enemy's squadron and, near the fort, to fire it with a slow match. Then they were to try and escape back to their countrymen, in a small boat. When it was night they hoisted their sails and the ship quietly started through the darkness, but before they had gone as far as they wished to get, among the enemy's boats, they were discovered from the fort and an alarm raised.

The great Decatur, with his comrades, stood gazing at the craft as it receded from them and the sails disappeared in the distance and darkness of the night. What must have been their feelings, as the noble ship disappeared? They were, no doubt thinking of their comrades, so brave, who might be going into the jaws of death. Could it be possible that they would never return, that they would never meet any more? They looked and listened, but they were gone, no sound of them could be heard. Awful suspense—all at once the fort opened fire on the brave crew. The light of their batteries brightened up the shore and the thunder of their cannon shook sea and earth. But where were the twelve Americans? Brave fellows, where were they? They had, no doubt, failed to get as far as they wished to, before they were discovered, and risked their lives a little too long. They applied the fire to the trail of powder and the ship was blown up. Tripoli had never been shaken before, nor had she ever witnessed such a sight. The flames shot up toward the sky; the whole city was illuminated and the report and awful force caused by the blowing up of the ship, made the enemy's vessels in the harbor heave to and fro, and rock as though in a storm. Men's hearts failed them; they did not know but that they were going to sink. The city itself was shaken to its foundation, from center to circumference. Men stood trembling and gazed with horror and astonishment. Not another cannon was fired, and the noise they made was no more when compared with the noise of the explosion, than the sound of a pop-gun compared to the sound of a cannon. In fact it was no comparison at all. Thousands stood ghastly and pale not knowing what the next moment might reveal. The proud Bashaw had been badly "shook up" and disturbed in his dreams of conquering the Americans. He had heard of the advance of William Eaton and he made up his mind that it was dangerous, for him, to carry on a war with beings who fought more like devils than men, so he concluded that he would go in for peace. The twelve brave men, who went with the fireship, were never heard of again. They returned to their comrades, to tell the thrilling story of their last adventure, never, no never. They had sold their lives, for their country, dearly. They were never to see their homes in North America, or their loved ones again; they had met their fate bravely and sacrificed their own lives for their country's glory.

Father also related the adventures and hardships that were encountered and overcome by William Eaton, who formed a union with Hamet, the elder brother and rightful heir to reign at Tripoli. Hamet had been driven from his country and family, wife and children, and was in hopes, by the aid of Eaton and the American war, of being reinstated at Tripoli. He joined with General Eaton, who had received his commission from the American government, and assumed the title of General. In conjunction with Hamet, he raised an army of twelve hundred men, adventurers of all nations, who volunteered to fight under the American flag. They started from Alexandria, in Egypt, and marched a thousand miles across the desert of Barca. They bore in their advance the American flag, something that had never been seen in that country before. After a tedious march they arrived at Derne, a city on the Mediterranean, belonging to Tripoli. General Eaton summoned the city to surrender. The Governor sent him this reply, "My head or yours." Then the American general drew up his men and rapidly advanced to attack the fort, which defended the city. He met with a strong resistance, the enemy numbering about three thousand. A terrible fire of musketry enveloped the combatants in fire and smoke. The voice of General Eaton, though he was wounded, was heard, amid the din of battle, encouraging his men.

After a severe contest of about two hours they charged and carried, by storm, the principal fort. They tore down the Tripolitan flag and ran up the stripes and stars in its place. This was the first time it had ever been raised over a fort on the Mediterranean Sea, or in fact the old world. General Eaton was fortifying, making the place stronger, receiving some volunteers, through the influence of Hamet, and preparing to march upon Tripoli to help the American fleet. But he was in need of supplies and every day was expecting to receive them.

As the city and harbor were under his control, he had everything in readiness for his march, excepting the supplies, when the American Frigate, the "Constitution," appeared and announced that peace was declared, 1805. The conditions were that Hamet should leave the country and his wife and children should be sent to him. The American prisoners were to be exchanged and the American seamen not to be compelled to pay tribute any more.

The Americans who had been enslaved by the government of Tripoli were to be paid for the labor they had performed. It is evident that the reigning Bashaw was alarmed for his own safety and was glad to compromise.

Father said it always grieved him to think, that the Americans who had been held as slaves at Tripoli never returned to their native home. They were paid for their service during the time they had been enslaved, went on board a ship, sailed for North America and were never heard of again. They slept the sleep of death with the twelve most brave beneath the dark cold waves, never more to see their families or friends.

Father often repeated such stories in our wilderness home in regard to this war, the revolutionary war and the war of 1812. I and the other children always listened to these tales with much attention and interest. It was the way I received most of my knowledge, in regard to such things, in those days. As we lived in the woods of Michigan my means of acquiring book-knowledge were very limited. Now, I believe, if I were to read the sum and substance of the same thing every month in the year, for years; the way he related those old stories would still be the accepted way to my mind. Although they might be clothed in language more precise and far more eloquent it would not appear so to me.

CHAPTER XXIV.

LIGHT BEGINS TO DAWN.

Father's farm improved with astonishing rapidity and became quite a pleasant place. Some of the stumps rotted out, some we tore out and some were burned up. In these ways many had disappeared and it began to look like old land. It was rich and productive and, in truth, it looked as level as a house floor. Some seasons it was rather wet, not being ditched sufficiently to take the water off. Yet father raised large crops of corn, potatoes, oats and wheat. Wheat grew very large but sometimes ran too much to straw; some seasons, rust would strike it and then the grain would shrink, but as that and gets older, and the more the clay is worked up with the soil, the better wheat it raises. In my opinion it will be as good wheat land as the oak openings or prairies of the West for all time to come.

Father built him a good frame barn and was getting along well. He bought him a nice pair of black horses which proved to be very good and serviceable. It began to seem like home to mother. She too possessed very good conversational powers. Her conversation was always accompanied with a style of frankness and goodness, peculiar to herself, which gained many friends, who became warmly attached to her, enjoyed her hospitality, witnessed her good cheer, as they gathered around her board and enjoyed luxuries, which in some of the years past we had not been able to procure. The learned and illiterate, the rich and the poor, shared alike her hospitality. No one ever asked for bread, at her door, who was refused, if she had it, even to the poor Indian. We had many comers and goers, and I think there were but few in the town of Dearborn who had more friends than father and mother.

Several years after we planted the first thirteen apple trees, father set out a little orchard of fifty trees, west of them. Some of these proved to be very good fruit and supplied us with better apples, of our own raising, (and in fact some earlier apples) than we had been used to getting from along the Rouge. Then it could be said of us that we sat under our own vine and apple tree and ate the fruit of our hands, without any one to molest us or make us afraid. And, it could be said of father, that he made the place, where the wilderness stood, to blossom as the rose. Everything seemed to work together for our good and all nature seemed more cheerful.

The evening breeze that kissed the rose and made the morning glory (that grew by our window) unfold its robe, so that it would be ready in the morning to display its beauty, and caused the sunflower, aided by the evening dew, to change its face so that it would be ready to look toward the sun, bore away on its wings, over the fields, the fragrance of the rose and the joyful songs of civilization. In the stillness of the beautiful evenings the air, under the starry canopy of heaven was made vocal with the songs and tunes of other days, which had been learned and sung oftimes before in a native land nearly eight hundred miles away.

Now the pioneer felt himself safe. He could retire to his bed, in his log house, and quietly rest in sleep, without draining any more of the redman's approach, or having by his own strong arm, to defend his family. Now he need have no fear of Mr. Bruin entering his pig pen and carrying off his pig, as he did ours one night some years before. He tore the hog so badly that it died, although it was rescued by father and his dog. The bear escaped to the woods. Now how changed the scene with us. We could retire and sleep soundly; feeling as secure as if we had gone to bed way down in the State of New York. We could leave the leather string of the door latch hanging out for any one to enter, as nearly all the early settlers were friends. The ax was now left stuck in the wood block on the wood pile. The rifle hung in its hooks, not to be disturbed. In other nights, of our first settlement, father did not feel safe; the string of the door latch was taken in, the door was fastened and blockaded on the inside, his ax and rifle were placed with care back of the curtains, at the head of his bed. None of us knew what might happen before the light of another morning, for we were in a wilderness land and neighbors were far apart. How different a few years have made it! Now nature seems to smile upon us and the evening, when it comes in its beauty, seems to offer us quiet and repose, rest and security. Now when nature puts on her sable habiliments of night, the blue canopy was covered with stars, that glistened and shone in their glory, as they looked down upon us and seemed to witness our prosperity. How they illumined our beautiful spring nights! The beautiful feathered songsters, that had returned from the south, warbled their songs in our ears anew and seemed to exert themselves, to make their notes clear, and let us know they had come. The little grey phebe-birds, the robins and the blue birds were the first harbingers of spring. As night put on its shade their little notes were hushed in the darkness, then the whip-poor-will took up the strain. He would come, circle around and over our house and door yard and then light down. He too came to visit us, he had found our place again. In fact, he found us every spring after we settled in Michigan, and cut out a little hole in the woods. At first his song seemed to be "whip-poor-will, whip-poor-will, whip-poor-will;" then, by listening, it could be made out to say, "good-will, good-will." In later years, by the aid of imagination, his notes were interpreted, "peace and plenty, peace and plenty." But, whatever we might imagine him to say, his song was always the same. He was a welcome visitor and songster, and his appearance in spring was always hailed with joy.

Sometimes I would rise early in the morning and go out of the door just at daylight. I could hear the notes of the little songsters, just waking, singing their first songs of the morning. I would listen to see if I could hear the gobbling of the wild turkeys. I hardly ever failed to hear them, sometimes in different directions. I frequently could hear two or three at once. The old gobblers commonly selected the largest trees, in the thickest woods, with limbs high up, for their roosts and as soon as it came daylight, in the east, they would be up strutting and gobbling.

They could be heard, in a still morning, for a mile or two. The gobbling of the turkey, the drumming of the partridge upon his log, the crowing of our and the neighbors' roosters and the noise of woodpeckers pounding the tops of old trees, were the principal sounds I could hear when I set out with my rifle in hand. I made my way through the prickly ash brush, sometimes getting my clothes torn and my hands and face scratched, when going into the dark woods in the early morning. I went for the nearest turkey that I heard, often wading through the water knee deep, the woods being nearly always wet in the spring.

If the turkey did not happen to be too far off and I got near it, before it was light, and got my eye on it, before it saw me and flew away, I would crawl up, and get behind some tree that came in range between me and it so that it could not see me. I had lo be careful not to step on a stick, as the breaking of a stick or any noise that I was liable to make would scare the turkey away. If I had the good luck to get up to that tree without his discovering me, I would sit or stand by it and look with one eye at the old turkey as he gobbled, strutted, spread his wings then drew them on the limb where he stood and turned himself around to listen and see if there was anything new for him to gobble at. If he heard the distant woodpecker, pounding away with his beak, on the old hollow top, he would stretch up his neck and gobble again as cheerfully as before. Then I would put my rifle up aside the tree to see if it was light enough for me to see the sights on it. If it was not I would have to take it down and wait a few minutes for it to get lighter.

I felt very uneasy and impatient, while waiting, and wanted to take that turkey, by the legs, and carry him home over my shoulder. When it was light enough so I thought it was dangerous to wait, as the turkey might discover me or fly off his perch then I would draw up my rifle, by the side of the tree, and shoot at him. Sometimes the old turkey would retain all his feathers, fly away and leave me, to wade back to the house, thinking to myself I had had a hard job for nothing. The great trouble in shooting wild turkeys on the roosts, in the spring of the year and in the early morning, is in not being able to see the sights on the rifle plain enough. Of course, I was sometimes rewarded, for my early rising and wet feet, by a nice turkey to take home to father and mother for dinner.

This style of hunting for the wild turkeys was known by the settlers in an early day. Another way I had of capturing the turkeys by shooting them, was by the use of a small instrument that I almost always carried in my vest pocket when in the woods. It was made from the hollow bone of a turkey's wing. I called it a turkey call. By holding the end of my hand and sucking it right, it would make a noise, or squeak, very similar to the turkey's voice. Sometimes, when I heard one gobbling in the woods, I would go as near as I could, and not let him see me, and hide myself behind an old log, or root, where a tree had been blown down, take the hollow bone out of my pocket and call. I have seen them come up on the run, sometimes one, at other times more. While lying in ambush once I shot two, at the same time, with one rifle bullet and got them both.

I have often shot at a flock, in the woods. They would scatter and fly in all directions. I would run ahead, near where I thought they lighted, hide and call. If a lone turkey heard the shrill note, he would answer and was easily decoyed up to me. In this way I was very sure to get him.

Father made one of the luckiest shots at wild turkeys of which I ever knew. They had a notion of coming into his buckwheat field and filling their crops with buckwheat, sometimes two or three times a day. Father discovered them in the field; he went away round and approached them from the woods, on the back side of the field, where they came in. The turkeys discovered him through the brush and fence and huddled up, with their heads together. He said they were just getting ready to fly. He shot amongst them, with a shot gun, and killed four at once. There are at the present time, 1875, scattering wild turkeys in the town of Dearborn, but they have mostly disappeared. Tame turkeys, in abundance, have long since taken their place.

CHAPTER XXV.

MAKING A BARGAIN.

When I was twenty-one we had a good young team, of our own, and father made it a rule to go to Detroit once in two weeks, with butter and eggs. When he had other farm products he went oftener. Every other Friday was his market day, for butter and eggs. His butter was contracted at Detroit by the season, for one shilling a pound, and father thought that did very well. By starting early, he could go and do his marketing and return by noon. How different from what it was when it took us two nights and a day, and sometimes more, to go to Detroit and back. Father had to sell his produce cheap; when we had commenced raising and had some to sell, all appeared to have an abundance to sell. Detroit market then seemed rather small not having its outlets for shipping, and everything we had to sell was cheap. We also bought cheap; we got good tea for fifty cents a pound, sugar was from six to ten cents per pound, and clothing much cheaper than it was when we came to Michigan.

We could buy brown sheeting for from six to eight cents per yard. Very different from what it was, when everything we bought was so dear, and when we had so little to buy with. One day father and I went to Detroit with a large load of oats. We drove on to the market and offered them for sale; eighteen cents a bushel was the highest offer we could get for them and father sold them for that price. We fattened some pork, took it to Detroit and sold it for twenty shillings per hundred. In days back, father had often paid one shilling a pound for pork and brought it home on his arm, in a basket over two miles. Now we were able to sell more than we had to buy. The balance of trade was in our favor and, of course, we were making some money; laying up some for a rainy day, or against the time of need.

I told father, as we had a good team, it would be handy if I got me a buggy. I could take mother at her pleasure, and it would be very handy for me to go around with, so I went and bought one. It was a double buggy with two seats. After the buggy was bought, when mother and my sisters wished to go to meeting or to visit friends, I would hitch up the team and take them in, what I thought, pretty good style. We had, what I called, a gay team and, in fact, a good rig for the woods of Michigan. I took care of the team, and when I went out with them I tried to make those horses shine. I trimmed their head stalls with red balls, as large as hens' eggs, and from them hung scarlet ribbons six inches long. When I came home in the evening between, sun down and dark, through the woods, the little blacks made the evening breeze fan my passengers and we left the little musical songsters in the shade. I now worked very hard and helped father all I could in fixing up his farm. He had everything around him that was necessary to make him and mother comfortable.

About this time I formed a more intimate acquaintance with a young lady, Miss Traviss, although her name was very familiar to me and sounded very beautifully in my ear, some how or other I wished to have it changed. After I made this acquaintance I thought I would go to Detroit and spend the next "Fourth" and see what they were doing there and try city life a little. As one of my sisters wanted to go I gave Miss Traviss an invitation to go with us, which invitation she accepted. So when the morning of the "Fourth" came, we started for town. We put up at the "Eagle Tavern" on Woodbridge street and spent the day very patriotically. We had what we thought a very splendid dinner. We had the first cherry pie that some of us had eaten since we came to Michigan. We visited all the sights we could hear of, and honored almost every display with our presence. When the salute of the day was fired, of course, we were there; they fired one big gun for Michigan. As the cannon thundered forth its fire and smoke, it seemed to fairly sweep the street with its tremendous force; it was terrible and grand. It seemed to bid defiance to all the world. It was the salute of the cannon of American freemen. We thought we would go over to Canada to see what was going on there. When we were across, we observed that the people didn't seem to be paying any attention to the "Fourth." But we felt very much like holding Independence and thought we would take a walk, down toward Sandwich. Of course, I was seeing all I could of Canada, but Miss Traviss took the greater part of my attention. The more I enjoyed her company, the more I thought, in view of future life, that it was necessary for me to make a private bargain with her.

After we had walked as far as we thought it was pleasant, we turned back toward Windsor; when we were nearly there we met a colored man. I pointed over the river toward Detroit, and asked him, saying, "What place is that yonder?" "Why," said he, "dat am die United States ob 'Merica ober dar." He answered me like a man, with frankness, supposing that I was a stranger to Detroit, and accompanied by beautiful young ladies of Canada he naturally supposed that I did not know the place. I left Canada thinking that all of the North American Continent ought to belong to the United States.

We sailed back to Detroit, the beautiful "City of the Straits." We all felt as though we were at home, in our own country and thanked our stars, that we did not live in Canada; that we lived in the land of the free, and that our flag, the old star-spangled banner, waved over "the home of the brave." We went back to the "Eagle Tavern;" I told the hostler I wanted my team. In a very few minutes he had it ready and we were on our way home, enjoying our evening ride. I was very attentive and vigilant, in the presence of my company.

When we were home we told our parents all the incidents of the day. We had had a good time and had enjoyed ourselves very much. Then I attended to hard work and farming, and think it would have been difficult to find a man, who would have performed more labor than I did until I was past twenty-two years old.

In the mean time, I was having an eye out and thinking of domestic affairs and life. I will not tell what old folks would call it, but I call it falling in love with Miss Traviss. I made a private bargain with her and got the consent of her father and mother, which was a hard job for me although they acquiesced willingly. It was also approved by my parents. We had it ratified by a minister and afterward I heard her called, by others, Mrs. William Nowlin. She had taken a new name upon herself. I left my father's home to build up one for myself and another, and never more to return to my father's house and call it my home.

CHAPTER XXVI.

HOW I COMMENCED FOR MYSELF— FATHER'S OLD FARM IN 1843.

When I commenced for myself, father gave me a strip across the two lots on the south end of his farm, south of the Ecorse, containing forty-two acres and lying on the town line between Dearborn and Taylor. Thus fulfilling (as far as I was concerned) what he had said long before; he wanted land for his children. I supposed, at the time, I should build a house, live there and make it my home. I had a chance to trade it off even, for eighty acres of land lying half a mile west of it, subject to a mortgage of one hundred and fifty dollars. I made the trade, paid the mortgage and afterward built on the place, the house in which I now live.

Father bought back the forty-two acres which he had given me, and he easily paid for it—two hundred and fifty dollars. Then he had the old farm together again, with money left, which he had saved by his frugality and industry. He made up his mind that he would buy another place, which was offered for sale, out one mile toward Dearbornville, beyond the clay road. It had a good barn on it and a comfortable farm house. He moved there in 1848 and lived on one of the most beautiful building places in the town of Dearborn and on the corner where three roads met.

About this time, my second sister became acquainted with a young man, by the name of Michael Nowlin, and married him. She was more lucky than most young ladies; she did not have to change her name, only from Miss to Mrs. Nowlin. She went with her husband to live near Romeo, Macomb County, Michigan. He was a farmer there. Father did not like to have one of his children so far away. I told him it would be well for him to let my brother-in-law and sister have ninety acres of the old farm, which would make them a good home. So he offered it to them, and they came and settled on it, and lived where I had lived so long before, with my father and mother, brother and sisters, in the woods of Michigan.

Father let them have it on easy terms, and gave Sarah what he considered was her portion as far as he was able. My brother-in-law easily met the payments, paid for his place and had a good farm. He, being a good business man, soon had his farm clear and things comfortable around him. But he was not entirety satisfied with the place, though it was the best of land, and he was a man capable of knowing and appreciating it. He thought he was laboring under some disadvantages. In the spring of the year the clay road was very bad and he had hard work to get out and in. School privileges were also poor, not such as he desired for his children, and he made up his mind to sell has place. He sold it in two parts, at a good advantage. The last piece for over a hundred dollars an acre. He bought him a nice house and lot in the city of Ypsilanti, is nicely situated there and has given his children a liberal education. So ninety acres, of what was once my father's old farm, were disposed of.

After I had left home, a few years passed and my brother, John Smith Nowlin, was married and started out in life for himself. Father let him have the west seventy acres of the old farm. He, being the youngest son, father desired to see him settled comfortably in life near him. He gave him the place so cheap and on such easy terms that he was able to pay for it in a short time, right off of the place, with the exception of what father gave him as his portion. Father said he gave him his part. He soon had as nice a little farm as any one need wish to own in the State of Michigan, and he had it clear from debt. After my brother-in-law moved away my brother became lonesome, dissatisfied and was not contented with so good a place. He sold it in two pieces and bought a farm out within half a mile of Dearbornville, beyond father's. He moved on to it and lives there now right in sight of the village.

It is not my intention to delineate, at any length, the circumstances of any of the family unless in connection, with my father and mother, or the old place where we first settled in the wilderness, where I labored so hard, in my young life, and took so much interest in my father's getting along during his trying days in the woods of Michigan.

I was along there, by what was father's old place, one day this winter, 1875. I looked at the barn and saw that it was getting old. I noticed the two little orchards, some of the trees had disappeared and others looked as if they were dying, with old age. I saw young orchards on the place, which were set out by other hands, those who knew but little of us. I thought things looked strange; that there was not one of the Nowlin name who owned a foot of the old farm. I suppose to this day no part of it, nor the whole of it, could be bought for less than one hundred dollars an acre, probably not for that.

I counted the dwelling houses that have been built on it, there are five of them; three very good frame houses, well painted and built in good style, the other two houses are not so nice. I noticed there were four good frame barns on it. The old place is inhabited by an industrious race of men. It is divided up into German farms.

Men may cover mother earth with deeds and mortgages, call her their own and live upon her bounty, little thinking of the hardships, toils and privations, that were endured by those who preceded them. How they labored, toiled and sweat, sometimes without enough to eat and not knowing where the next meal was coming from. I know this was the case with some of the first settlers.

In view of the hardships and sufferings of the pioneer and his passing away, I exclaim in the language of another, "This earth is but a great inn, evacuated and replenished by troops of succeeding pilgrims."

"One generation passeth away and another generation cometh, and man here hath no continuing city."

[NOTE.—Since this was written, I have learned that I made a slight mistake in regard to the forty-two acres, of the old farm, which father gave me, as it passed through other hands before my brother and brother-in-law came in possession of it; but it was finally divided as I have stated.]

CHAPTER XXVII.

THOUGHTS IN CONNECTION WITH FATHER AND EARLY PIONEER LIFE.

I follow father, in my mind, to his last farm which he bought in 1849, where he lived out his days. It was not cleared up, as he wished to have it, and he continued to labor as hard as ever before, trying to fix it up to suit him and to get it in the right shape for his comfort and convenience. The soil was as good as the place he left. He raised large crops on it. One day I went to father's and inquired for him. Mother said he was down in the field cutting corn. I went to him; he had a splendid field of corn and was cutting it up. The sweat was running off from him. I told him it was not necessary for him to work so hard and asked him to let me take his corn-cutter, as though I was going to cut corn. He handed it to me, then I said I am going to keep this corn-cutter: I want you to hear to me. Let us go to the house and get some one else, to cut the corn; so we went to the house together.

But it was impossible for me or anybody else to keep him from hard labor, although he had plenty. He had become so inured to hard work that it seemed he could not stop. He finally got all of his farm cleared that he wanted cleared. A few of the last years of his eventful life, he let some of his land to be worked on shares and kept his meadow land and pasture. He needed all of that, for he kept quite a stock of cattle, sheep and horses and took care of them himself, most of the time, up to his last sickness.

He was a great lover of good books; and spent much of his leisure time reading. He did not often refer to the hardships which he had endured in Michigan; but often spoke of the privations and endurance of others. Thus, in his latter days, not thinking of what he had done, he seemed to feast on the idea, that America had produced such and such ones, who had been benefactors and effectual workers for the good of our race.

Most of those men who came here in the prime of life, about the time that father came, are gone. The country shows what they have done, but few consider it properly. Some know what it was then and what it is now and know also, that it has arrived at the exalted position it now occupies through the iron will, clear brain and the steady unflinching nerve of others. Yet they pass on in their giddy whirl and the constant excitement of the nineteenth century, when wealth is piled at their doors, and hardly think of their silent benefactors.

Who can think of what they have done and not feel their heart beat high with gratitude, admiration and love to the Giver of all good, in that he ever raised up Such glorious people as some of the Michigan pioneers were? So enduring, so self-sacrificing, so noble—in fact, every element necessary to make beings almost perfect seemed concentrated in them. I do not say it would be right, for me to wish the pioneer to live forever here, and labor and toil as is the common lot of man. He might be surrounded by friends and loved ones and plenty of this world's goods, and have time to look back upon his past life and see what he had been through and accomplished. He had gone into the forest, built him a house, cleared up a farm, and lived where a white man had never lived before.

I would say to him as Daniel said, 2426 years ago, to King Darius, who visited, very early in the morning, the cavern where he was confined. The king asked him, in a mournful voice, if his God, whom he served, had been able to deliver him. Daniel said, "O King, live forever!" It has been the belief of good men, in all ages of the world, that they were going to have a better and happier existence in the future after this life had passed away. Darius had spent a restless and sleepless night fasting.

No instruments of music were brought into his presence, his mind was too much troubled thinking of the prophet, who lay in the lions' den. Thinking how his faithful servant had been divested of his scarlet robe, golden chain and office, and might be devoured by the lions. In the early gray of the morning the king hurried to the cavern and cried out in a sorrowful voice to his friend and said, "Daniel, O Daniel, servant of the living God, is thy God, whom thou servest continually, able to deliver thee from the lions?" Daniel answered the king and said, "O King, live forever. My God hath sent his angel, and hath shut the lions' mouths." Daniel was aware that the King wished him no evil, but had set his heart on him to deliver him and that he had labored hard to save him. He knew, that the king had been caught in a snare which was set for him by the crafty princes. That he had been persuaded by them to sign a decree, which according to law could not be changed. It was gotten up, through jealousy and envy, for the purpose of taking Daniel's life. When Daniel heard the doleful voice of the king, calling him, he answered, and with an honest heart exclaimed; "O King, live forever!"

This was not wishing, as some might suppose, that the king might live forever, on the earth, in his natural or mortal state, or forever reign over his kingdom in this world, but this acclamation was "Live forever." As it was evident he could not live long in this world, Daniel wished him a better existence in a future state.

Man has not been able to find, in this world, the land of perpetual youth or spring of life. Nearly all the veteran pioneers, who have fought with the forests of Michigan, and labored for themselves and others, until they grew old, and wrinkled and their heads were silvered o'er with gray, have passed from the storms of life.

They failed to find such a land as Ponce de Leon, looked for in Florida, in the year 1512. He was so delighted with the variegated flowers, wild roses, ever green and beautiful foliage, and the fragrance of the air, that he thought that these woods must contain the fountain of life and youth and that that must be the place upon the earth where men could live and never grow old.

When I was quite young, a few years after our settlement, I think in 1838, Mr. Elijah Lord came and settled about a mile and a half north-west of father's. He came down with his oxen by father's place to get small, hard-maple trees, out of the woods, that he wanted to take home and set out on his place. He was then about a middle-aged man. He set out the trees on both sides of the road, running through his place, for about eighty rods, in front of his house. I asked him if he expected to see them grow up; he said he did not set them out for himself, but for the benefit of other people, for the good of the generations that would follow him.

Some years after that, I visited Mr. Lord in his last sickness. He looked very much older than he did when he planted the trees. He looked careworn and sad; his locks were gray and he was very feeble. He was fighting his last battle of life and he soon went to that bourne, whence no traveler returns. He was a good man, a deacon of the Presbyterian church at Dearbornville at the time of his death.

The hard maple trees, which he set out, are grown up to be large trees. When leaved out, they have the most beautiful tops, with the most perfect symmetry that could be imagined. They make splendid shade for the road. In summer weather, when the rays of the sun were very hot, thousands have enjoyed walking under their protecting boughs. The poor horses and cattle that travel that road alike enjoy the benefit of those trees. The farmer as he is going or coming from market and stops his team, to rest under their shade, enjoys their cooling and refreshing influence. The pedestrian, who sits down by the fence to rest his weary limbs, takes off his hat and with his handkerchief, wipes the perspiration from his brow, as he fans himself with his hat talks to his neighbor about the price of things and the beautiful shade, that is around and over them. Neither of them know anything about the benevolent man, who over thirty-five years before set out the maple trees, whose shade they enjoy and which protects them, from the scorching rays of the sun, and makes them so comfortable.

Now, in looking at the shortness of human life, which is compared to a hand's breadth or to the vapor, which appears in the morning is seen but a little while and then vanishes away to be seen no more; and thinking that the pioneers stopped but so short a time to enjoy the fruits of their toil and the labor of their hands, I would exclaim again in language similar to that of the good man of old, "O, pioneers, pioneers, live forever!"

O, why should the spirit of mortal be proud?
Like a swift fleeting meteor, a fast-flying cloud,
A flash of the lightning, a break of the wave,
Man passes from life to his rest in the grave.

The leaves of the oak and the willow shall fade,
Be scattered around and together be laid;
And the young and the old, and the low and the high,
Shall moulder to dust and together shall lie.

So the multitude goes, like the flowers or the weed
That withers away to let others succeed;
So the multitude comes, even those we behold,
To report every tale that has often been told.

For we are the same our fathers have been;
We see the same sights our fathers have seen;
We drink the same stream, and view the same sun,
And run the same course our fathers have run.

The thoughts we are thinking our fathers would think;
From the death we are shrinking our fathers would shrink;
To the life we are clinging they also would cling;
But it speeds for us all like a bird on the wing.

Yea! hope and despondency, pleasure and pain,
We mingle together in sunshine and rain;
And the smiles and the tears, the song and the dirge.
Still follow each other, like surge upon surge.

'Tis the wink of an eye, 'tis the draught of a breath,
From the blossom of health to the paleness of death,
From the gilded saloon to the bier and the shroud,
O, why should the spirit of mortal be proud?

—Selected.

It appears to me that it will be interesting to men, who in the future shall live along the Ecorce and enjoy their beautiful homes and farms, to know who were the brave, sacrificing, benovolent men who first settled the country, and were a few of the many who have made the State of Michigan what it will be to them.

I give together the names of some of those early worthies whom I have mentioned before in this sketch. They were the first settlers of the southeast part of the town of Dearborn. Their names are arranged according to the time of their settlement along and near the Ecorce with the years and seasons of their settlement in the wilderness.

>Joseph Pardee—Fall of 1833.
>John Nowlin—Spring of 1834.
>Asa Blare—Fall of 1834.
>Henry Traviss—Summer of 1835.
>George Purdy—Fall of 1835.
>Elijah Lord, about—1837 or 1838

Let these bright names be imperishable! Let them be indelibly written, in letters of gold, on leaves as white as snow and live in the light. Let them be handed down through future ages, in the archives and annals of the country, until the end of time.

Of the six, whom I have mentioned here, only one survives. That one is Mr. George Purdy. He lives on the Ecorce yet and owns a good farm. (1875.)

Recently a wise man said to me: "We can engrave the names of our kindred and the friends of humanity upon stately monuments of marble and they will crumble to dust, be obliterated and rubbed out by the hand of time; but, if inscribed upon the flat surface of a written page, their names will live."

Men of all ages have delighted to honor their heroes and to perpetuate their names. It is right to give honor to whom honor is due. We cannot tell how many of the names of the good and great of the earth's true philanthropists were engraven upon tablets of dead stone, who have long since been forgotten and the knowledge of them lost in the past.

The blight—mildew—blackness and creeping moss of time have hidden their names from earth. How few, in comparison to the many, have been handed down to us in history.

CHAPTER XXVIII.

FATHER'S NEW HOUSE AND ITS SITUATION—HIS CHILDREN VISIT HIM.

I have said that I tried to persuade father to take life more easily and not to labor so hard himself on the new place he had bought. It was a new place to him; but in an early day it was the oldest place south of Dearbornville. The first log house built south of Dearbornville, in the town of Dearborn was built on it by John Blare in the year 1832 or 1833. It was one mile south of Dearbornville. So there was a house standing there when we were slowly making our way to Michigan. When we came, it was the first house south of Dearbornville. Mr. Joseph Pardee, who crossed Lake Erie, with his family, the fall before when father came viewing, built his house a mile south of that. These two houses were the first ones, south of the village of Dearborn, in the town of Dearborn. When we came in and built, our bark covered house was the next.

It was at this house of Mr. J. Blare that the Indian, John Williams, threw his knife on the floor and commanded Asa Blare to pick it up. There he sat in his chair, flourished his knife, looked at its frightful edge and told what it had done. If the Indian told the truth, it had cleaved the locks and taken off the scalps of six of the Anglo Saxon race—some body's loved ones. It had been six times red with human gore, and was going to be used again, to take off one more scalp, one of the few who was then in the woods.

This house of Mr. Blare's had long since been torn down and had disappeared. I could now go within five rods, and I think less, of where the house stood. When Mr. Mather bought the place he built him a frame house across the road, beyond where Blaire's house stood. It was built on a hill, on five acres of ground, that he owned there by itself as a building spot.

Mather sold these two places to Barnard and Windsor and father bought the places of them, and moved into the Mather house. Father talked, from an early day, that when he got able to build a house, he would like to build it of brick or stone. He said if he had stone, he could build a house for himself. I have no doubt that he would have built his house himself, if he had had the stone, as old as he was, when he got the money to do it with.

He thought himself quite a stone mason, at least he thought he could lay a stone wall as strong as any one. I stated that I had seen where he had built stone walls. The walls I had reference to then were walls for fence. I saw where he had built one large out door stone cellar and arched it over with stone; I also saw where he had built a smaller one, that opened into what was styled a cellar kitchen. He also built the three walls of the kitchen, on the back side and two ends, of stone; the front of the house being wood.

The practice of laying stone, in his early life, made him want to build him a stone house in Michigan. If he had settled in another part of Michigan, he might have done it; but he found that stone were hard to get here, being too far away. So he made up his mind, he would build him a brick house. He said brick buildings were safer, in regard to fire, and were more durable, that they did not require so much repairing, were warmer in winter and cooler in summer than wooden buildings.

So he went at it, and built him a good, substantial plain, brick farm-house in 1854. Not so palatial as some might admire, but a good substantial house; a brick basement under the whole of it, with two stories above. He set it right facing the "Hard scrabble road" and right in front of his door yard was the junction of three roads. He lived on the corners and, by looking south, he could see to the place where he first settled in Michigan, from his own door. He built across the front side of his house a double stoop or piazza, running the whole length of the front. There he could sit, in the cool of the day, and rest himself, accompanied by some of his family. Two of my sisters yet lived at home; the rest of the family had gone for themselves. While sitting there he could see people passing and repassing, coming and going in every direction. What a contrast it was to our early life in Michigan. Now he could sit on his veranda in the twilight, when it was pleasant, and when the shadows of evening were spread over the face of nature, he could peer away into the distance to the south and southwest, for a mile and more, and see lights in different places glistening and shining like stars through the darkness. They were the lights of lamps and candles, burning in his distant neighbors' dwellings and shining through their windows. He could go to his north window and see lights all along, from his house to Dearbornville, for he was in plain sight of the village. Now he lived in what might be styled, if not an old country, a thickly inhabited part of the country.

A few years before, when father and I were out and could not get home until after dark, we frequently walked through the woods a mile or two without seeing a light. When we came to our clearing we could see one light, and that was mother's lone light in the window waiting for us. It was three or four years, after we settled in Michigan, before the light of any neighbor's window could be seen, from our house. Father's situation was very different when he was comfortably settled in his new house. When he had it built he told me that he lacked a very little of paying for it. I asked him how much he needed. He said, "Not more than a hundred dollars." I told him I could let him have it as well as not. So I gave it to him and he sat down and wrote me a note of a hundred dollars, ten per cent interest per annum. I told him I didn't want any note. He said I must take it if he took the money. So I took the note, looked at it, saw that it was upon interest and told him that I would not take any interest of him. But I took the note home and laid it away. I was pleased to think that father had so good a house and was so well situated. He built him a very strong house and located it upon a commanding eminence overlooking the country in every direction. From its very solid appearance shortly after it was built it was called "Nowlin Castle;" it is now known to many by that name.

Father and mother enjoyed their new home very much. They usually invited their children, and their companions home all together once in a year or two. They often got into their carriage and rode down to see me and I was always glad to see them. I usually counseled and consulted with father when I thought of transacting any business of importance.

After a year or two father spoke to me about the hundred dollars; I told him I didn't want it, that he could keep it just as long as he wanted it, until he could pay it just as well as not and it wouldn't cost him any interest.

Time passed on until about five years were counted after father built, when he came down one day, on foot, to see me. He brought in his hand a little leather bag of silver money—mostly half dollars. He said he had come down to pay me that note, that he didn't need the money at all and wanted me to take it out of his way. I looked up the note, sat down by the table, turned out the money and counted it. I saw there were just fifty dollars; then I looked at the note and saw it had been given about five years before.

I told father that I had said I shouldn't take any interest of him, but it had run so long, I didn't know but what it would be right, for me to have the interest. I couldn't quite afford to give so much. The fifty dollars was just enough to pay the interest and I could endorse it on the back of the note. I turned a little in my chair, to look at father, as he sat off at one side and said but little to me, to see what I could make out in mind reading. I found that I failed; I could not make out, by what he said nor by his silence, what he thought of me. Then I told him, that I had a little job or two on hand, which I wanted him to help me about. I asked him it he would help me. He said he would if I didn't bother him too much. I told him I wanted him to have his stoop painted over, it would preserve and make the wood last longer, and make it look better. And I wanted him to go to Detroit for me, as soon as he could conveniently, and get some oysters, and other good things, and bring home with him. Then I wanted him to invite all of his children to come and take dinner with him and mother and enjoy the day together. Besides, I wanted him to take the fifty dollars, toward paying the expenses, and also take that note out of my way, toward what I was owing him.

In a few days after that I was invited up to the castle to spend the day. We were all there, father, mother, brother, sister, and our companions. We had a good dinner. The table was spread with the bounties of life. We passed a very pleasant day, and listened to father's stories of wars, and stories connected with his early life. He would relate them as nobody else could. He told us stories that I had often heard him relate before. Still there was a charm in his manner of telling them and they seemed to be always good and new; his old stories were certainly as attractive, interesting and pleasing as ever before.

It would make almost any one laugh who listened to them, though he always looked rather grave while repeating them. It pleased him to think that they all enjoyed them so much; but what pleased him still more was that his children were all alive at home. As they were most all singers, sometimes, he would set them singing for him, songs new and old, as he was no singer himself.

Mother was a beautiful singer. He often got her to sing for him, and sometimes asked her to sing his favorite song, which was styled "The Star in The East." I have heard her sing it for him, at different times, ever since as long ago as I can remember hearing her sing. It was a beautiful piece, connected with the Messiah's advent, which happened over eighteen hundred years before. One verse of it was this:

> "Cold on his cradle the dew drops were shining,
> Low lies his head, with the beasts of the stall;
> Angels adore him in slumber reclining,
> Maker and Monarch and Savior of all."

It is claimed by some, that the human voice is capable of producing more different sounds and is more musical and pleasing to the ear than anything else earthly; that it is but little below the seraphic strains. "The Star in The East" referred back to the most glorious night, for the human race, that earth ever knew. A multitude of the heavenly hosts came down in the east of Judea; the darkness of night was driven away and the place became more beautiful than day, for glory shone around them. They announced to the wise men of the East, that the Savior of mankind was upon the earth, and that he was at Bethlehem. They told them how and where they would find him. The Heavenly visitors showed them a star or meteor of exceeding brilliancy and told them it would conduct them to the place where he was. They started with the star in advance; it lighted their path and conducted them to the place. There was heard sung, that night, one of the most heavenly, beautiful, thrilling and enchanting songs that ever broke upon the ear of mortal men. It was sung by angels, this was their song: "Glory to God in the highest, and on earth peace, good will toward men." Then the bright messengers plumed their pinions, spread out their snow white wings, filled up their shining train and in a cloud of glory flew away to Heaven.

Now as I have strayed a little in thinking of the subject of "The Star in The East" I find myself back again in the presence of the one who sung father's favorite song.

I told mother she must get ready, and, in the fall, we would go back to the state of New York. I asked father to go with us, and tried to get him to say he would go. But he thought he would have to stay at home and take care of things while we were gone. Mother concluded she would go and said she would get ready for the journey and we would go and see the old native places, and old friends and make the visit we had talked about so long. The thought of Lake Erie had always been a dread to mother, whenever we spoke of going back. But now we could go back very easily and in a very short time with the cars on the "Great Western Railway" I told her it would be as easy, for her, as though she were sitting in a parlor. I encouraged her all I could, for she was getting quite old and feeble, and it looked like a big undertaking to her. I said, to encourage her, that she would be able to stand it first rate, and the trip, no doubt, would do her good. I think the thought of going was pleasing to her.

But we met not many more times at my father's house, under so favorable and happy circumstances, nor gathered around his board with everything in such good cheer, and prospects so bright.

CHAPTER XXIX.

MY WATCH LOST AND VISIT TO CANADA.

Mother's maiden name was Melinda Light. Her mother died when she was quite young. She and father were married when she was about nineteen years old. She took one of her youngest brothers to live with her, and she acted more the part of a mother than a sister to him. She sent him to school and gave him a good education. His name was Allen Light and he was thoroughly qualified to officiate in the capacity of a pedagogue. He taught a number of terms, prudently saved his wages and bought father's little farm, before we left the state of New York. He married a young woman, who had some capital of her own, before we came away, and they settled on father's old place, and lived there when we came to Michigan. For this uncle I did some of my first working out, mostly picking up stone; he gave me a shilling a day. I worked for him until I had, what I thought was quite a purse of money and I brought some of it to Michigan.

As father lived in a hired house I had my own time, during my vacations when I was not going to school. One man was quite displeased with me, because I refused to work for him for sixpence a day. Another man for whom I did work in haying, and spread hay after two or three mowers and raked after, never paid me anything. I supposed he would give me eighteen cents or two shillings a day. I worked for him four days; he was a rich man at that time. I wanted father to ask him for it for me, but he said if the man wasn't a mind to pay it let him go.

Thirty years afterward, when I was there, I met the same man, he was riding a horse down a hill as we were going up. I asked my cousin who he was and when he told me I remembered the work I had done for him. I inquired, of my cousin, about his circumstances; he said that he used to be a rich man, but that he had lost his property and was poor. I am sure, I didn't feel much like sympathizing with him.

Uncle Allen wrote to mother very often after she came to Michigan. He told her how much he missed her, that she had been a mother to him. He said the doors of the house, as he turned them on their hinges, seemed to mourn her absence. It was this brother and his family that we wanted to see the most. We heard from him often and learned that he had been successful in business. He bought two farms, joining the one he bought of father, and one about a mile off and paid for them, they were farms which father and mother knew very well. We learned, from others, that he was a wealthy, prominent and influential man, in that old country. Fickle fortune had smiled on him and he had taken what she offered to give. In the fall we were going to see them. The war of the rebellion had commenced, 1861, when we got ready to go and see them.

Some three or four years before this I hired three or four colored men, who came from Canada, to work for me. The right name of one of them, I think I never knew, it was necessary for him to keep it to himself. Campbell and Obadiah were the names of the other two.

The people of the United States, both North and South, were very much excited, at that time, upon the subject of slavery. The Government had passed a law, in favor of the South, thundering forth its penalties against any one who should aid or harbor, feed or employ one who was a fugitive slave. That law required northern men to turn out when notified, leave their business, help to hunt and chase the fugitive down, capture him and help to put on his fetters. So it was not for me to know the name of the one, who had been recently a slave.

Campbell had a considerable confidence in me and told me a little of the history of the escaped slave, (some things I knew already); that when he ran away, from the land of bondage, he was guided in his flight by the north star. The slave had heard of Canada and knew if he could reach that country he would own himself and be a free man. If he ever had a family his wife and children would be his, and would not be owned by any one else. They would belong to himself and not another. To gain his freedom he traveled mostly nights. When he came to a creek or river, if he couldn't find a bridge or boat, he either swam or waded across. While on his journey he subsisted on fruit or grain, anything he could get hold of. When he saw it was coming light, in the morning, he would select him a place a little way from the road, if he happened to be in one, in a swamp or woods, or any place that offered him a hiding spot, and there spend the day sleeping or watching. When everything was quiet in the evening he would come out of his hiding place, set his face toward the north and hurry on. He was trying to leave his master as fast as possible, and every night he was making the distance greater between them. Sometimes, when he reached the road, he would stop and listen to see if he could hear the sound of horses' hoofs, or men approaching him, or the shrill yelp of the blood hounds, that might have discovered his whereabouts or been on his tracks. If he heard nothing to alarm him he hastened on. Sometimes he was bare-footed and bare-headed, with no one to pity him, or know the anguish of his heart, but his Creator.

When night had spread her mantle over him, and the innumerable stars appeared, sprinkled over the vault of heaven, millions of miles away, all joined together to shower down upon the poor fugitive slave their rays of light. The faithful old north star, with its light beckoned him on to freedom until he got among friends and was safely taken, by the underground railroad, into Canada.

So I knew these colored men, while working for me, had some fear that one of them, at least, might be arrested and taken back into slavery. They didn't feel safe in working so far from Canada. But I am sure if I had heard of his master's approach, or his agent's, I should have conducted him, or the three, six miles, through the woods, to Detroit River, procured a boat and sent them across to Canada, regretting the existence of the "Fugitive Slave Law," and obeying a higher law.

As I have said I hired these three, from Canada, to help me through my haying and harvesting. I also gave them some other jobs. I relate this circumstance as it comes in connection with mother's visit to the East and what I said to my uncle there.

The names of two of these men were Campbell and Obadiah, as I have already stated, and these were all the names I ever knew for them. Campbell was an oldish man, and I found him to be very much of a man, trusty, ingenious and faithful in everything he did for me. Obadiah was a young man. He told me his parents died when he was young, that he had a sister younger than himself and a brother still younger. He said that he wanted to keep them together and provide them a home. This young woman kept house for my three workmen. She frequently came down to our house and helped Mrs. Nowlin. She seemed to be very nice and smart and had access to our house.

After I had finished my haying and harvesting they moved back to what, I think, was styled the "Reservation" in Canada, near Windsor. A short time after they were gone I missed my watch. It was kept hanging up in my room. It had unaccountably disappeared and seemed to be gone. I made up my mind, after all of my kindness to the colored people, that the girl had taken my watch and given it to her brother, Obadiah, or that at least he knew something about it, and that they had carried it to Canada. I wanted my watch and hated to lose it; what made it seem worse was its being taken from me under such circumstances. I made up my mind that I could contrive to get it again.

I went out to Dearborn, saw the Deputy-Sheriff of Wayne County, Daniel D. Tompkins, told him the circumstances and what my suspicions were, and my plan, and asked him if he would go with me to Canada. He said he would. I told him that I would come out with my team, he and I would go to Canada and decoy Obadiah across the river, have the papers ready and arrest him in Detroit. I had made up my mind that he had the watch or knew its whereabouts. I thought he would be glad to give it up in order to get out of the scrape, and all I wanted was, somehow, to get my watch.

Accordingly, in the morning I took my team and we started, went to Detroit, drove down to the wharf and waited for the large ferry boat to come to her wharf. Mr. Tompkins was a shrewd man. He thought that he would cross on the little ferry boat, that was then in, and see what he could learn on the other side, and got aboard and went over. While I was waiting I spoke to a mulatto and asked him if he was acquainted in Canada, and what they called the reservation back of Windsor, three or four miles. I told him I wanted to find a man by the name of Campbell. (I thought I should be able to find Campbell as he was the oldest man and he would be able to tell me where Obadiah was.) The mulatto asked me what his given name was. I told him I didn't know, I always called him Campbell. He said there were two men by the name of Campbell there; they were brothers and one of them was a preacher. I told him I thought one of them was the man I wanted to see. He stepped back by the corner of a saloon and commenced talking with another colored man privately; soon another one joined them, and there were three. I noticed them, as they cast sly glances at me, and I thought they were making some remarks about me, or my rig. I had a large team hitched to a covered carriage, double-seated. I led my horses on to the ferry boat, and when it started, two of the colored men stepped aboard. We went across to Canada, I led my horses on to the wharf and found my comrade there waiting for me. I asked him if he had found out where they lived; he said not. We got into the carriage and started for the reservation, being sure that no one knew anything about our business but ourselves, however, I thought, from what I had seen, that things appeared rather suspicious.

We drove up the river road. There was another road running back farther from the river, into the country, which also led to the reservation.

We drove along a pretty good jog for a mile or two, and who should we meet but the old man Campbell! He seemed very glad to see me, and came right up to shake hands with me. He wondered how I came to be in Canada, and inquired very particularly about the health of my family. I asked him where Obadiah was, told him I wanted to see him. He pointed across the road and said, that he came down with him and stopped there to get an ax helve. Said he would run in and tell him, that I had come, and in a minute out they came; Obadiah laughing and looking wonderfully pleased to see me. Of course I had to appear friendly, although I didn't feel very well pleased. I supposed that I would have to wear two faces that day; but I was spared the disagreeable task. I told Campbell and Obadiah, that I had come over to see them, that I had a little job on hand which I wanted to have done and that if they would go to Detroit with me I would tell them about it. They said they would go and I told them to get into the carriage. They said they could walk, they were afraid of soiling it; I told them to tumble in and I would take them to Windsor in a few minutes.

While we were talking up came a colored man on horseback, his horse upon the jump, breathing as if he had rode him fast. He spoke to Campbell and took him one side and talked with him. Then Campbell stepped back to me laughing and told me what the man said. He said: "Heaps of colored people" thought I was a "Kentuckian;" they said, I looked like one and that my team and carriage looked like a Kentucky rig. The man would not believe but that I was one, and thought that I had come to get a colored woman, who had been a slave in Kentucky; and he said, that there was a great excitement among the colored people about it.

I learned something of the circumstance; that woman had been a slave in Kentucky. Her master thought a great deal of her, treated her with much kindness, in fact made quite a lady of her and gave her liberties and privileges, which thousands of other slaves never enjoyed. But she made up her mind, that she wouldn't be the property of any one; her life should be her own. She ran away to Canada to gain her liberty. When she arrived there, she didn't find every thing as pleasant as she had expected and expressed a willingness to return to her master and slavery, in the land of bondage. Through a secret agent, her master had learned where she was. He made a bargain with the preacher, Campbell, to get her back. He was to have quite a sum of money if he succeeded in persuading her to return to her master.

The colored people had found it out and every man of them branded the preacher Campbell, as a traitor and enemy to his race. They were watching him and the colored woman, and were determined, that no one who had gained their liberty should ever be subjected to slavery again, if they could prevent it.

Campbell and Obadiah got into the carriage. By this time we had convinced the first trooper, that I actually was a Michigan man (for he saw for himself, that I had no woman) and we started back toward Windsor. We shortly after met another horseman following up; when he met us he turned with us. They had alarmed all of the colored people on the road and nearly every man had volunteered for duty. They told us that some men had gone on the other road, on horse back, to cut us off in case we turned that way.

I began to make up my mind that, sure enough some how or other, we had raised quite an excitement among the colored people. We were attended by quite a cortege. They seemed to be paying a good deal of attention to a couple of Michigan men. We had attendants on foot and on horse back, before and behind, and we were quietly making our way toward Windsor. If persons, who did not know us, and knew nothing of the affair or circumstance, had stood in the main street in Windsor, opposite the ferry, and seen us come in, attended by our retinue, they might have thought, that I, a Michigan farmer, had the King of the Sandwich Islands accompanied by some great Mogul, that I was their driver and that the Deputy Sheriff, of Wayne County, Michigan, was their footman.

When we came up opposite the ferry, the crowd of colored men was so great, we had to stop and give an account of ourselves. They had raised the alarm in Detroit and she had furnished her quota of colored men for the emergency. The excitement had helped the ferry business a little.

We found ourselves surrounded by a large concourse of people. I told them, that I did not know anything about the woman nor of Kentucky. Some of them wouldn't believe but what there was actually a woman in the carriage and they had to step up and look in and examine it, in order to satisfy themselves. Luckily, some of those who came across from Detroit knew me and knew that I was no Southerner.

Campbell was my main spokesman. He was a very sensible man and more than an average talker. He said: "Why gemman, I know this man well; he libs in Dearbu'n. I worked for him heaps of times, often been to his house. We're goin to Detroit wid him to see 'bout a job."

One colored man, more suspicious than the rest, crowded his way through up to the carriage, opened the door, took Obadiah by the arm and told him to get out, that he wouldn't let him go across; he said he was a young man and it was dangerous for him to go over. Obadiah said that he knew "Misser Nowlin fust rate," that he had worked for him and that he had more work for him to do and he must go over. Other men, who knew me, reasoned the case with them, and they finally concluded it was a false alarm, closed the carriage door and we were permitted to drive on to the ferry. We soon crossed back to Detroit; to what some of the colored people considered so dangerous a place for their race.

I had Campbell hold the horses while my friend, Mr. Tompkins, and I consulted together concerning Obadiah. I told my friend, that I hadn't been able to detect any guilt in Obadiah from the first to the last. I thought if he had been guilty he would have been alarmed, and have allowed himself to have been taken out of the carriage in Windsor, and would not have crossed the river with us. Mr. Tompkins had made up his mind to the same thing. T stepped back to them and said, that I had consulted with my friend and changed my mind, that I wouldn't do anything about the job then. I have no doubt, they thought the colored people had raised such an excitement it had discouraged me and cheated them out of a job. (It is seen that the job I wished done just then, was to get my watch, and I had thought that Obadiah was the one who could help me accomplish it.) I told them, some other time when I had work I would employ them, and I did employ Campbell a number of times after that. I gave them money to get them some dinner and to pay their passage back, as I had paid it over. I left them feeling first rate; they never knew the object of my visit. They must have thought that I treated them with a great deal of respect.

When I reached home at night my pocket book was a little lighter, my trip had cost me something. I told my folks that if they had made out in Canada, that I was a southern man and that I was after that woman, it would have been doubtful about my ever getting home and that it would have taken three hundred Michigan troops to have gotten us out of Windsor, dead or alive. But I do say to exonerate those colored people from all suspicion, in the affair, that, some time after, the watch was found, nicely wrapped up in a piece of cloth and in a bureau drawer, where it had been laid away carefully and forgotten.

CHAPTER XXX.

MOTHER'S VISIT TO THE EAST—1861.

I go with her, accompanied by my wife and brother John S. As the train we wished to take did not stop at Dearborn I had a hired man, with my team, take us to Detroit. Father went with us to Detroit and to the Michigan Central Depot. We went aboard the railroad ferry boat and were soon across the river and on the cars on the "Great Western Railway." We were soon receding very fast from Michigan; going across lots and down through the woods of Upper Canada. I tried to see as much as I could of the country, while we were swiftly passing through it. I told mother we would manage it so as to see the whole route, either going or coming, by daylight. I didn't see anything in particular to admire in Canada until we got down near London and beyond. Then I saw some good country and I thought it would compare favorably with Michigan land.

Just before sundown we got to the swinging bridge, which hangs over and across Niagara River. We crossed it very carefully. Just as the sun was about half hid beyond the Western horizon our car reached terra-firma in the state of New York. I felt a little more secure and at home, than I felt when leaving Canada, when we had reached our native state.

In a little while we were aboard the cars of the "New York Central Railroad" and making our way through the darkness rapidly, toward the east. I told mother we must try and get a good rest, that night, on the way to Albany. We located ourselves the best we could for the night. We had only gone a little ways when, all at once, there was a terrible rattling and jingling, made by the passing of another train. It made a noise something like the shelf of a crockery store tumbling down and breaking in pieces glass ware, earthen ware and all. This noise was accompanied with a heavy rumbling sound which shook the ground and the car we were in and caused them to tremble. The flash of the light of the passing train, as it sped on its way, was so quick by us that it was impossible to see whether it was a light or not. It appeared like the ghost of a light or a spectre in its flight through the darkness, for a moment and it was gone. It left no trace behind that I could see. There had two or three of those trains of cars passed us before I was able to make out what made the extra noise. Not having any knowledge that there was a double track there, and never having rode where there was one before, it took me a little while, to make up my mind in regard to it.

Both trains going at full speed, in the night, the one we passed vanishing so quickly, yet not taking the impression it made on us with its whizzing, hissing, tearing sound, it seemed like some fierce demon from Tartarus bent on an errand of annihilation. But it was only another train, like unto the one we were enjoying, and, if as successful as the officers of the "New York Central Railroad" wished, it would only seem to annihilate time for its transient occupants. For the coal miner's invention seemed to make as much discount on time as any wonder of the last age except our American Morse' lightning talker. We found there was but very little sleep or rest for us that night. I could look out of the car window and peer into the darkness and see lights dotted along here and there; every once in a while, they seemed low down and looked some like the lights from the back windows of low log cabins. I made out that they were lights on board of canal boats. I recollected having passed along there about thirty years before, and that I jumped into the canal and got terribly wet. Now we were traveling at a more rapid rate; yes, as far in one hour as we did in all day then, with a large train of passengers. It was impossible for mother to get any rest that night. Just as it got nicely light, in the morning, we arrived at Albany.

No doubt there were on that train, who rode through the night with us, the churchman, the statesman, the officer and men who would quickly dress themselves in blue and march, under the old flag to defend our country. Farmers and mechanics, men and women of almost every station in life were there. Some went one way and some another, each intent upon what they thought concerned them most at the time.

We went to a restaurant for breakfast and especially to get a good cup of tea for mother. (It had been rather a tedious night for her.) Then we went on board a ferry boat and crossed over the North River, then took the "Harlem Railroad" for Pattison, where we arrived about noon. This was within three miles of where mother was brought up and I was born. We hired a livery team to take us to Uncle Allen Light's. In going we passed by a school house where I learned my "A, B, Abs."

Mother's heart beat high with emotions of joy as she neared her much beloved brother's dwelling. She had always thought of him as the young man she left thirty years before; but she found that the frosts of thirty winters had changed his locks as well as hers.

I asked the driver if Allen Light was much of a farmer; he said that he was. I asked him if he kept a good many cattle; he said he did. I told him when he got there to let the valises remain in the carriage, and to cover them up, after we got out, with the robes so they would not be seen, and that I wanted him to wait a little while, and I would try and buy uncle's fat cattle. At least, I would sound him a little and see what kind of mettle he was made of, and he would see the result. I made a special bargain with mother and she promised to keep still and keep her veil over her face until I introduced her. She told me afterward, she never would make another such a bargain as that with me. She said, it was too hard work for her, when she saw them to keep from speaking.

Just before we made this visit, my brother and I went to see friends west, and viewed some prairies of Illinois. We visited Chicago, the great city of the West, went through it where we saw a great deal of it. We went into the City Hall, or Court House, and up its winding stairs to a height so great, that we could overlook most of the city. I saw that the city covered a good deal of ground. From the elevated position we were occupying, we looked down and saw men and women walking, in the street below us, and they looked like a diminutive race. As I looked I thought the ground was rather flat and level for a city, but we made up our minds it was a, great place. Some of the merchandise of all the world was there. We came home feeling very well satisfied with our own city, Detroit. For the beauty of its scenery and the location of the city I should give my preference to the "City of the Straits."

Now I had gotten away down east. I had rode a little ways on the outside of Cowper's wheel. We had all got out of the carriage, in front of uncle's house, went up to the door and knocked and all went in. I asked if Mr. Light lived there. Uncle said he was the man. Aunt brought chairs for the ladies and they sat down. She asked them if they would take off their things, they refused, as much as to say, they were not going to stop but a few minutes. I asked uncle immediately, if he had some fat cattle to sell. He said he had some oxen that he would sell, and we went out to look at them. Of course I was more anxious to see how uncle appeared than I was to see the cattle. They were in the barnyard near the house. I tried to make uncle think, that I had cattle on the brain the most of anything. I walked around them, viewed them, felt of them, started them along, asked uncle how much they would weigh, &c. I kept a sly eye on uncle, to see how much in earnest he was and how he looked. He was a portly, splendid looking man. He appeared, to me, to be a good, hale, healthy, honest farmer, well kept and one who enjoyed life. He would sell his property if he got his price, not otherwise. He was rather austere and independent about it. He asked me my name and where I was from. (This is a trait of eastern men, down near Connecticut, to ask a man his name and where he lives and, sometimes, where he is going.) I saw that uncle was getting me in rather close quarters, but I talked away as fast as possible, walking around and looking at the cattle. I asked him what he would take for them, by the lump, I was trying to evade the questions, that he had asked me.

I told him that my home was wherever I happened to be, that I paid the cash for every thing which I bought, that I had just come from Illinois, where I had relatives, and down through Michigan. I told him that I was very well acquainted in some parts of Michigan, that I had been in Canada and that a great many people there called me a "Kentuckian;" and I didn't know as it mattered what I was called so long as I was able to pay him for his cattle. I wanted to know the least he would take for them; he told me. Then I said, I would consider it, we would go to the house and see how the ladies were getting along.

Going along I made up my mind that uncle thought I was rather an eccentric drover. He seemed to be interested in what I had said about Michigan and wanted to know something about the country. When we went into the house, I saw that mother was getting impatient and our livery driver sat there yet, waiting to hear how it came out and to deliver our satchels.

Mr. Light, your name sounds very familiar to me, I have heard the name, Light, often before. Have you any relatives living in the West? He said he had two sisters living in Michigan, in the town of Dearborn. Why, said I, I have been in the town often and am well acquainted there I know a good many of the people. It is ten miles west of Detroit on the Chicago road. I saw he began to take great interest in what I said. I asked if he thought he would know one of his sisters if she were present. He said he thought he would. I told him there was one there.

Then they threw off all restraint and met as only loved ones can after so long a separation. Uncle was overjoyed to see her again, upon earth, and mother was delighted to see him and Aunt Betsey. The light of other days, youth and happy associations of life flashed up before them in memory clear and vivid, which touched the most sensitive chord of their hearts and caused them to vibrate, in love for one another. They visited as only two who love so well and have been separated so long can visit. Minds less sensitive, than theirs, cannot imagine with what degree of intensity of spirit and feeling, they told over to each other, first some of the scenes of their youth, which they enjoyed together so many years before, then the absence of loved ones dear to them both. A father, two brothers and a sister had departed their life since mother moved to Michigan. Ah! what changes thirty years had produced! Their voices, which mother had heard so often there, she never would hear again and the smile of their countenances would never greet her more. They were gone and their places left vacant. A great many former acquaintances of mother had also disappeared. They talked about the hardships they had endured while apart and of some things they had enjoyed which were as bright spots, or oases, in the desert of their separation.

Now as I was there, I wished to visit the place where I had been in days of yore, in my childhood. The places had changed some but I could go to every place I remembered. The distance, from one place to another, didn't seem more than half as far as I had it laid out in my mind.

The country appeared very rough to me. What we used to call hills, looked to me like small mountains. I supposed the reason was because I had been living so long in a level country. The rocks and stones appeared larger and the stones seemed to lie thicker on the ground than I had supposed. The ledges and boulders appeared very strange to me I had been gone so long. I found that the land was very natural for grass, where it wasn't too stony. It produced excellent pasture upon the hillsides, good meadow on the bottom and ridges, where it was smooth enough and not so stony but that it could be mowed.

I went to see our old spring. It was running yet. Uncle had plenty of fruit. I looked for the apple trees that I used to know and they had almost entirely disappeared. I saw where they had raised good corn and potatoes on uncle's place. Oats, that season, had been a very poor crop. Wheat, uncle said they couldn't raise, but they could raise good crops of rye. I passed by another school house where I had attended school. The same building where I got one pretty warm whipping for failing to get a lesson. The school buildings which I saw there both looked old and dilapidated. I thought they looked poor in comparison to our common school houses in Michigan. I had a good many cousins, who lived there; scattered around. I went to see as many of them as I could. I had one cousin, who lived off about four or five miles. I wished very much to see her for I remembered her quite well, we were young together. Uncle's folks said she was married and lived on a ridge that they named. Cousin Allen said he would go with me to see her, so we started. Before we got there we had about a mile to go up hill. Cousin got along very well and didn't seem to mind it, but it was up hill business for me to climb that ridge. I wondered how teams could get up and down safely; they must have understood ascending and descending better than our Michigan teams or, it seemed to me, they would have got into trouble. We finally got on to the top of what they called a ridge. I found some pretty nice table land up there, for that country, and two or three farms. After we reached the highest part of the ridge we stopped and I looked off at the scenery, it appeared wild and strange. I could look north and see miles beyond where uncle lived and see hills and ridges. I could look in every direction and the same strange sights met my view. I think my cousin told me, that to the southwest of us, we could see some of the mountains near the North river. While I looked at the rugged face of the country, it didn't seem hardly possible that that could be so old a country, and Michigan so new.

West of us we could look down into a hollow or valley. The flat appeared to be about eighty rods wide, on the bottom between the ridges. West of the hollow there arose another great ridge, like unto the one on which we stood. Along this hollow there was a creek and a road running lengthwise with the hollow. I saw a man, with a lumber wagon and horses, driving along the road; from where I stood, and looked at them, they didn't appear larger than Tom Thumb and his Shetland ponies.

We finally got to my cousin's, I found that she had changed from a little girl to an elderly woman. She was very glad to see me and wanted me to stay longer than I felt inclined to, for I wanted to be back to the old home again, viewing the scenes of my childhood as, to me, there was a sort of fascination about them.

Up there I noticed a small lake, near the top of the ridge. I thought it a strange place for a lake. I asked cousin if there were fish in it, he said there were, that they caught them there sometimes. I asked if the lake was deep; he said in some parts of it they could not find bottom. I looked over it away down into the hollow beyond, and thought there might be room enough below for it to be bottomless; it might head in China for all I knew. As I gazed I thought, can it be possible that this country appears so much rougher, to me, than it used to, and yet be the same? As I stood and peered away from one mountain and hill to another, at the gray and sunburnt rocks, jagged ledges, precipices and the second growth of scrubby timber, that dotted here and there and grew on the sides of hills, where it was too stony and steep for cultivation, it astonished me.

My friends appeared well pleased with their native hills and vales and I have no doubt they thought, as they expressed it to me, that they lived near the best market and that New York was ahead. But the place how changed to me! If I could have seen some wigwams and their half nude inhabitants, on the hill sides, in the room of the houses of white men, and have witnessed the waving of the feathery plume of the red man, above his long black hair, I should have thought, from the view and the face of the land, that that old country was very new and wild and that Michigan, where I lived at least, was the old country after all.

Nature seemed to be reversing the two countries. It appeared to me like the wild—wild—west Yosemite valley and mountains, or some other place. How strange! Here I am standing upon my native soil. I used to think it was the brightest spot upon this dim place men call earth.

In coming down the hill, I had to be cautious how far I stepped, in order to keep upright, as I was liable to move too fast, get up too much motion, I had to hold back on myself and keep one knee at a time crooked. In that way I got safely down. I was a little cautious, for I had on me scars made by falling on stones and cutting myself, when near that place long years before, when I was a little boy driving father's cows, to and fro, night and morning, from the new place he bought, (the buying of which was one great reason of our going to Michigan to find a new home and live where white men had never lived before.)

I went back to uncle's and told him, that I had made him a pretty good visit. I tried to get him and some of the rest of my friends to promise me to go west and see our country and judge of it for themselves. They said we western men had to bring our produce, and whatever we had to sell, down to the New York market, in order to dispose of it. I made up my mind, if New York was the head and mouth of Uncle Sam, that his body and heart were in the great central West, his hands upon the treasury at Washington and his feet were of California, like unto polished gold, washed by the surf of the Pacific Ocean. When Uncle Sam wished them wiped he could easily place them on his snow topped foot-stool, the Rocky mountains, and Miss Columbia, with a smile would wipe them with the clouds and dry them in the winds of the Nevada, while she pillowed his head softly on the great metropolis, New York, where the Atlantic breeze fans his brow and lets him recline in his glory, the most rapidly risen representation of a great nation that the world has ever seen.

When Uncle Sam brings his hand from Washington it is full of green backs and gold, which he scatters broadcast among his subjects. Here and there across the continent it flies, like the leaves in autumn, so that it can be gathered by persevering men, who till the soil or follow other pursuits of industry. It is free for all who will get it honestly.

A little east and north of the garden city, is Michigan, one of Uncle Sam's gardens. I think it is a beautiful place, dotted here and there and nearly surrounded by great fountains that sparkle, glimmer and shine, in the sun, like the rays of the morning—beautiful garden. It is interspersed, here and there, with groves of primeval evergreens and crossed now and then by beautiful valleys and dotted by flowery walks and pleasant homes of the gardeners. It abounds in picturesque scenery, has a very productive soil and helps to furnish some of Uncle Sam's family, of about forty millions, with many of the good things of life, even down in "Gotham." So we get some of their money, from down there, if they are ahead of us and the head of America. I am satisfied for one, to live in one of the peninsula gardens of the West.

As my wife wished to visit her native place on the Hudson River, we would have to stop there a short time, and as my wife and brother wished to visit the city of New York we bade good by to uncle and his family and started. Took the "Harlem Railroad" and in a short time were in the city. We put up at the "Lovejoy Hotel" opposite the City Hall. We had rooms and everything comfortable. We visited the Washington market and some of the ships that lay in the harbor. We went on board one ocean steamer, went through it and examined it. We crossed the river to Brooklyn. Visited Greenwood Cemetery and saw all the sights we could conveniently, on that side of the river. One night we visited Barnum's American Museum, after this we went to see the Central Park and other places. We made up our minds that we had seen a good deal and that New York was an immense city.

CHAPTER XXXI.

LEAVING NEW YORK CITY FOR HOME.

We thought it was about time we started for home. We began to want to get back to Michigan, so we agreed to start. Brother J. S. was to take the "Harlem Railroad," go to uncle's, stop and visit, get mother and meet us, on a certain day at Albany. My wife and I took the "Hudson River Railroad" and came as far as Peekskill. We visited together the place of her nativity, where she lived until she was twelve years old. She found many very warm friends there among her relatives. We passed through Peekskill hollow to visit some of her friends. There I saw some beautiful land. It looked nice enough for western land, if it had not been for the rugged scenery around it.

When the day came, that we were to meet mother at Albany, we took the cars and started. When we passed Fishkill I knew the place well. I had been there a number of times before, when I was a boy. Newburg, on the opposite side of the river, appeared the most natural of any place I had seen. Along the river it appeared beautiful, and the mountains grand. It was the first time I had been there since we moved to Michigan. We soon passed Poughkeepsie, the place where we took the night boat, so many years before, bound for the territory of Michigan.

As we approached the Catskill mountains, I should say ten or fifteen miles away, they looked like a dark cloud stretched across the horizon; and when we came nearer and nearer the highest one, and it was in plain sight, it appeared majestic and grand. From the car window, we could see the mountain house that stood upon its towering summit. We could see small clouds, floating along by the top of the mountain. That was the greatest mountain I had ever seen; yet it is small in comparison to some in our own country. Not one third so high in the world as Fremont's peak, where he unfurled the banner of our country, threw it to the breeze and it proudly floated in the wind, higher than it had ever been before.

We soon got to Albany, went to a hotel near the railroad depot, called for a room and told the landlord that we would occupy it until the next morning. As mother could not rest on the cars, I thought it would be easier for her to stay there over night, and we would see some of the western part of the state of New York the next day.

After dinner we locked up our room and Mrs. Nowlin and I went out to take a look at Albany. We went up to the state house, the capitol, and visited the room, where the legislators of the "Empire state" meet to make laws for her people. There we saw the statue of the extraordinary man, Secretary of State and statesman, William H. Seward. He, who shortly after, was attacked by an assassin, where he lay sick upon his bed, in his room at Washington and was so severely wounded, that the nation despaired of his life for some time.

We went back to the hotel, and as the time was nearly up for the Harlem train from New York City, I went back across the river to meet mother and brother John Smith. The train shortly came in and they had come. Brother had mother upon his arm. She was very glad to see me. I got hold of her and she had two strong arms of her boys to lean upon. I told her we had a room over in Albany and were keeping house; that we would stop there all night and start again in the morning. It would make it more easy for her, and we would not have those jingling, rattling cars passing in the night, to keep us awake. We crossed over the river and went to our quarters. We four were all together again and had some new things to tell each other as we had been apart a few days. We passed the night very comfortably.

Early the next morning a regiment of soldiers, from the west, came hurrying on to the seat of war to defend the flag of our Country and the glorious Union. It rained very hard, I stood one side and noticed the "Boys in Blue" as they came pouring out of the depot. Their officers did not seem to have them under very good control. Their discipline wasn't very good yet; after they got out, there were several of them who seemed to be inclined to go on their own hooks. The officers had about all they could do to keep them along. One physically powerful, hardy looking man passed near me. He said, he thought it was a little hard, early in the morning, after a fellow had been jammed and bruised all night and it rained that he couldn't be allowed to stop and take a drop. The officer told him to keep in the ranks. I felt interested to know if they were Michigan men, but was not able to learn where they were from.

In a few minutes we were aboard of our train and started again for Michigan. The prospect of getting home soon elated mother very much. She had lost most of her attachment for her native place, and it was no comparison, in her mind, to her Michigan. She said uncle offered to give her a farm, if she would move back there and spend the remainder of her days by him. But it was nothing in comparison to Michigan, it was an inducement far too small for her to consider favorably. We were coming home as fast as steam could bring us and it was raining all the time. I told mother I thought we should run out from under the rain clouds before night, but that was a mistake. It rained all day long and was dark when we got to the suspension bridge. When we got off the cars, the runners were a great annoyance to mother. I told her not to pay any attention to them, we would find a good place. There was a gentleman standing near us, who heard what I said. He told me that there was a good house, the "New York Hotel," which stood close by. Said he was not interested for any, but that that house was a good one. I told mother we would go there and we started. I was helping mother along and told my wife and brother to follow us. It was hard work for them to get away from the runners. They hated very much to give them up, and they were making as much noise over them as a flock of wild geese. But my wife and brother left them and followed us. We got to the "New York House" and called for a room. We found it to be a very good house. We wanted to stay over night there, as it would be better for mother and we wished to go up and see the Falls next day. The next morning after breakfast my wife, brother and I went up to the Falls. As it was still raining mother stayed in her room, she didn't wish to go.

We went up on the American side and went down three hundred steps of stairs to the foot of the Falls. After this we viewed Goat Island, went across it to the stone tower, went up its rickety winding stairs to the top and looked upon the majestic scenery of nature, which was spread out before us there. I saw no place there where it appeared so terribly grand to me as it did when I stood at the foot of the Falls. There we went out on the rocks as far as we could, and not get too wet with the spray, and viewed the water as it poured over the cataract and plunged into the abyss below, beat itself into foam and spray, which settled together again and formed the angry waves that went rolling and tumbling away to the sea. There I heard the sound of many waters thundering in their fall and I thought, while looking at that sublime and wonderful display of nature, that the waters of the river and creeks of my own "Peninsula State," after turning hundreds of mills, slaking thirst and giving life to both man and beast, came there for an outlet. It plunges into Niagara River and goes gliding away to the ocean; some of it to be picked up by the wind and rays of the sun and rise in vapor. When formed into clouds in the atmosphere it is borne back on the wings of the wind, condensed by the cold air and falls in copious showers of rain upon the earth, to purify the atmosphere, moisten and fertilize the fields and cause vegetation to spring forth in its beauty. The rain falling upon the just and the unjust makes the heart of the husbandman leap for joy, at the prospect of a bountiful harvest, causes the foliage and the gardens to put on a more beautiful green, the lilies of the valley and the rose in the garden ("the transient stars of earth") to unfold themselves more beautifully. Then the cloud passes away, bearing and sprinkling the limpid fluid upon other lands, and the sun looks out upon the cool, healthful, invigorating and refreshing scene. The beautiful rainbow, in its splendor, seems to span the arch of heaven, placed there as a token of remembrance, so long before. It lasts but a little while and then disappears, the cloud also passes away. In this and similar ways the rivers and creeks are kept supplied with water and the Falls of Niagara kept continually roaring.

We went back to the "New York House" and shortly after took the cars for Dearborn. We arrived there about ten o'clock in the evening. Mother walked home, to the "Castle," a mile, very spryly. She seemed to feel first rate. She was pleased to get home. Father and the family had retired for the night when we got there, but father soon had a light and a fire and was ready to listen to our stories. We told him how near we had come losing mother. That uncle had offered to give her a farm if she would come back, live on it and spend her days by him. We told him what farm it was; he knew the place as he was well acquainted in that country. We told him if she went back they could go together and he could carry on the farm. But the inducement was far too small for them to entertain the thought of going, for a moment. Michigan was their home, had won their affections and was their favorite place.

I told father, that he must go and visit his native place, see how rough it was and I would go with him. I thought it would appear rougher to him than he expected or could imagine. He said he would like to go back sometime and see the country once more. He kept putting it off from year to year. It is said, "Procrastination is the thief of time." He never went. He bought him eight acres more land joining his two places. He paid for it seventy dollars an acre and had some money left.

Part of the eight acres was a ridge covered with chestnut trees. Father enjoyed himself there very much, a few of the last falls of his life, picking up chestnuts. He was a man a little over six feet tall. He walked straight and erect until the sickness, which terminated his existence in time, at the age of seventy-six years, in the year 1869. He went the way of all the earth. The rest of the family and I, missed him very much. Our counselor and one of our best friends was gone. He had fought his last battle and finished his course.

Mother survived him. She gave each of the children a silver piece (they were all old coins of different nations and times, each worth a dollar or more) which father had saved in an early day. They were in mother's work basket in the dark room at Buffalo, were brought in it, through the fearful storm on Lake Erie, to Michigan and saved through all of our hard times in the wilderness. I have my piece yet, as a keepsake, and I think my brother and sisters have theirs. After father's death, mother still lived at the "Castle" and my sister Bessie, who took all the care of her in her old age that was possible, stayed with her. All the rest of the children did every thing they could for her comfort. She felt lonesome without father, with whom she had spent nearly fifty years of her life. She lived a little over three years after he was gone and followed him. She was seventy-one years old, in 1873, when her voice was hushed in death and mother too was gone.

We laid her by father's side in a place selected by himself for that purpose. It is a beautiful place, about a mile and a half southwest of where they lived and in plain sight of what was their home.

Long before this there was a voice of one often heard in prayer in the wilderness, where we first settled, and that voice was mother's. Father and mother believed in one faith and mother from her youth. For years they tried to walk hand in hand, in the straight and narrow path, looking for and hastening to a better country than they had been able to find on this mundane sphere.

CPSIA information can be obtained
at www.ICGtesting.com
Printed in the USA
LVHW05s0119021018
592105LV00020B/1754/P